# MASTERS OF FANTASY

Five of the greatest writers of fantasy-adventure present five of their most famous heroes, in thrilling stories selected for your pleasure by Hans Stefan Santesson, former editor of *Fantastic Universe* and *The Saint Mystery Magazine*, and well-known anthologist. Meet them now, the heroes and the authors!

CONAN—Robert E. Howard
ELAK—Henry Kuttner
THONGOR—Lin Carter
SUAR PEIAL—L. Sprague de Camp
THE GRAY MOUSER—Fritz Leiber

**For Tore—**
**who introduced me to**
**Alexander Dumas almost**
**fifty years ago . . .**

# THE MIGHTY BARBARIANS

## GREAT SWORD AND SORCERY HEROES

Edited by Hans Stefan Santesson

LANCER BOOKS 🐴 NEW YORK

A LANCER BOOK • 1969

THE MIGHTY BARBARIANS
GREAT SWORD AND SORCERY HEROES

A WITCH SHALL BE BORN by Robert E. Howard. Originally
published in *Weird Tales* for December 1934. Copyright © 1934 by
Popular Fiction Publishing Company. Published by permission of
Mr. Glenn Lord, of Pasadena, Texas, literary agent for the estate
of the late Robert E. Howard.

DRAGON MOON by Henry Kuttner. Originally published in *Weird
Tales* for January 1941. Copyright © 1940 by Weird Tales, Inc.
Renewed 1968. Reprinted by permission of Harold Matson Com-
pany, Inc., literary agent for the estate of the late Henry Kuttner.

WHEN THE SEA KING'S AWAY by Fritz Leiber. Originally published in *Fantastic Science Fiction Stories* for May 1960. Copyright © 1960 by Ziff Davis Publishing Company. Reprinted by permission of the author and the author's agent, Robert P. Mills, Ltd.

THE STRONGER SPELL by L. Sprague de Camp. Originally published in *Fantasy Fiction* for November 1953. Copyright © 1953
by Future Publications, Inc. Reprinted by permission of the author.

THIEVES OF ZANGABAL by Lin Carter. An original story, published by permission of the author and the author's agent, Henry
Morrison, Inc.

LANCER BOOKS, INC. • 1560 BROADWAY
NEW YORK, N.Y. 10036

# CONTENTS

*Introduction*

LOOK at the world around you—today, this evening, or whenever you have the courage to do so with clear eyes —and you may understand why William Morris retreated into "worlds of his own invention," to use Lin Carter's phrase in his admirable study of Tolkien, *and* the attraction to this day of stories of adventure in almost-lands, such as these which you will find in this anthology.

William Morris—Edward John Moreton Drax Plunkett, Lord Dunsany—Eric Rücker Eddison—and particularly John Ronald Reuel Tolkien—each drew upon the folk memories of the past in creating their particular fantasy worlds within which you could lose yourselves, as they must have done at times, with a quiet prayer of thankfulness that even in these comparatively heathen times the hero-saga had not been allowed to wither and to die.

The urge to add to the known worlds is an urge as old as man, and antedates his first faltering steps taken into the then unknown. Romances have been rhymed, and only later written, about that unknown—about the monsters and the strange beings and the riches and the marvels and the miseries which it was certain must exist out there.

7

Over the centuries—over the millennia—the adventures of known and remembered men became the hero-sagas, sung or recited over leaping fires, exhortations to the young to in some measure equal the achievements of these heroes, warning to the common enemy that the traditions of the singers were the traditions of men of giant stature and of incredible valor.

Throughout the Middle Ages and into the infinitely more complex years we know as the Renaissance we see variants of this hero-saga, with political and social satire, masquerading as fantasy, more recognizable as such than in earlier days. Fantasy became a tool through the use of which alternate worlds could be portrayed which bore only a superficial resemblance to the grimmer reality. Very much as in later times, when in the years preceding the French Revolution, and, for that matter, still more recently, dilettante intellectuals could mock at the past and at the present, in allegorical fantasies and pageants dedicated to a complaisant Establishment, running scared when what they had written and what they had preached helped to destroy the world they knew.

Make no mistake about this: fantasy is a dangerous weapon in the hand of the accomplished political satirist, largely because there is no period of history in which there is no injustice, if not in the eyes of those Above, most certainly in the eyes of the Beholder. Each generation—each culture—thus births its own protest writers, as often from the mass as from the ranks of the Establishment of the day. It is worth noting though that these writers may often live long and honored lives, their fantasies remembered and thrilled to as blithely and as blandly, and as blindly, as when the *jongleurs* of the Middle Ages sang the praises of long ignored ideals . . . or Snorre Sturleson rewrote the history of his ancestors.

We are concerned here however with a subgenre of these folk tales which have lived through to our times in the writings of Tolkien and still others who have, with care and with affection, created alternate worlds in which we can take refuge for a brief while from the Orwellian realities which surround us.

Sword-and-sorcery stories: extrapolations from the known and the half-known, recreations of long-forgotten worlds which we have reason to believe existed in the long distant past, but of which nothing remains, nothing tangible, nothing which can be touched or felt or weighed in the hand. Nothing but that intangible something within the memory of the race which it is easy enough to dismiss as a folk myth if, in common with most people, you know nothing of history—yours and that of those who came before you.

We know by now that civilizations have risen and fallen and vanished into the mists of time on this world of ours. We know by now that the ancients, or those whom we call ancients, knew more about the past and those forgotten empires than we do, or will ever do. It is hard for us to face the possibility that ours is not the greatest civilization to have existed on this world. To acknowledge even the possibility of this demands a humility, and a sense of history, to which we are alien.

The adventure stories in this anthology, by Lin Carter, L. Sprague de Camp, Robert Howard, Henry Kuttner and Fritz Leiber, ignoring for the moment their pure entertainment value, hint at these possible worlds before the cataclysm which we are beginning to suspect did exist, and which we have reason to believe did at least have the color and the vividness and the cruelty and the action with which we now credit the late Middle Ages.

The worlds of Conan, of Elak, of Thongor and still others, thus reflect our unreadiness to credit these lost civilizations with the powers and the attainments which we feel are uniquely and solely ours, notwithstanding the use of magic by the protagonists. We are after all coming around (or aren't we?) to accepting the possibility that the word magic simply represents the exercising of powers forgotten but never quite lost by man. What we must now do, though, is to explore the possibility that these lost civilizations had in fact mastered the elements, and knew the stars.

As in time we may also know them.

But now, come with us to these worlds which Conan and the others knew. . . .

HANS STEFAN SANTESSON

*Judith Merril spoke for all of us when she paid tribute to Fritz Lieber in her introduction to his* The Secret Songs *(London: Hart-Davis, 1968), and told how for the past thirty years he has entertained, inspired, irritated, enlightened and delighted a "growing audience for fantasy and speculative fiction." You must have read his novel, A SPECTRE IS HAUNTING TEXAS, just published by Walker. Now read (or reread) this Fafhrd-and-Mouser story. . . .*

# WHEN THE SEA KING'S AWAY

## by Fritz Leiber

# WHEN THE SEA KING'S AWAY

STRIPPED to his loincloth, underbelt, and with amulet pouch a-dangle under his chin, the Gray Mouser stretched lizard-like along the bowsprit of the sloop *Black Treasurer* and stared straight down into the hole in the sea. Sunlight unstrained by slightest wisp of cloud beat hotly on his deep-tanned back, but his belly was cold with the magic of the thing.

All round about, the Inner Sea lay calm as a lake of mercury in the cellar of a wizard's castle. No ripple came from the unbounded horizon to south, east and north, nor rebounded from the endless vertically fluted curtain of creamy rock that rose a bowshot to the west and was a good three bowshots high, which the Mouser and Fafhrd had only yesterday climbed and atop which they had made a frightening discovery. The Mouser could have thought of those matters, or of the dismal fact that they were becalmed with little food and less water (and a ta-booed cask of brandy) a weary sail west from Ool Hrusp, the last civilized port on this coast—or uncivil-ized either. He could have wondered about the seductive singing that had seemed to come from the sea last night, as of female voices softly improvising on the themes of waves hissing against sand, gurgling melodiously among rocks, and screaming wind-driven against icy coasts. Or he could perhaps best have pondered on Fafhrd's madness of yesterday afternoon, when the large Northerner had suddenly started to babble dogmatically about finding for himself and the Mouser "girls under the sea" and had even begun to trim his beard and brush out his brown otterskin tunic and polish his best male costume jewelry so as to be properly attired to receive the submarine girls and arouse their desires. There was an old Simorgyan legend, Fafhrd had insisted, according to which, on the seventh day of the seventh moon of the seventh year of the Sevens-Cycle, the king of the sea journeyed to the other end of the earth, leaving his opalescently beautiful green wives and faintly silver-scaled slim concubines free to find them lovers if they could . . . and this, Fafhrd had stridently asserted, he knew by the spectral calm and other occult tokens, was the place of the sea king's home and the eve of the day!

In vain had the Mouser pointed out to him that they had not sighted an even faintly feminine-looking fish in days, that there were absolutely no islets or beaches in view suitable for commerce with mermaids or for the sun-bathing and primping of loreleis, that there were no black hulks whatever of wrecked pirate ships drifting about that might conceivably have fair captives imprisoned below decks and so technically "under the sea," that the region beyond the deceptive curtain-wall of creamy rock was the last from which one could expect girls to come, that—to sum it up—the *Black Treasurer* had not fetched the faintest sort of girl-blink either to starboard or larboard for weeks. Fafhrd had simply replied with crushing conviction that the sea king's girls were there down below, that they were now preparing a magic channel or passageway whereby air-breathers might visit them, and

14

that the Mouser had better be ready like himself to hasten when the summons came.

The Mouser had thought that the heat and dazzle of the unremitting sun—together with the sudden intense yearnings normal to all sailormen long at sea—must have deranged Fafhrd, and he had dug up from the hold and unsuccessfully coaxed the Northerner to wear a wide-brimmed hat and slitted ice-goggles. It had been a great relief to the Mouser when Fafhrd had fallen into a profound sleep with the coming of night, though then the illusion—or reality—of the sweet siren-singing had come to trouble his own tranquility.

Yes, the Mouser might well have thought of any of these matters, Fafhrd's prophetic utterances in particular, while he lay poised but unsweating in the hot sun along the stout bowsprit of the *Black Treasurer*, yet the fact is that he had mind only for the jade marvel so close that he could almost reach down a hand and touch the beginning of it.

It is well to approach all miracles and wonders by gradual stages or degrees, and we can do this by examining another aspect of the glassy seascape of which the Mouser also might well have been thinking—but wasn't.

Although untroubled by swell, wavelet, or faintest ripple or quiver, the Inner Sea around the sloop was not perfectly flat. Here and there, scatteredly, it was dimpled with small depressions about the size and shape of shallow saucers, as if giant invisible featherweight water-beetles were standing about on it—though the dimples were not arranged in any six-legged or four-legged or even tripod patterns. Moreover, a slim stalk of air seemed to go down from the center of each dimple for an indefinite distance into the water, quite like the tiny whirlpool that sometimes forms when the turquoise plug is pulled in the brimful golden bathtub of the Queen of the East (or the

15

drain unstoppered in a bathtub of any humbler material belonging to any lowlier person)—except that there was no whirling of water in this case and the air-stalks were not twisted and knotted but straight, as though scores of slim-bladed rapiers with guards like shallow saucers but all as invisible as air had been plunged at random into the motionless waters around the *Black Treasurer*. Or as though a sparse forest of invisible lily pads with straight invisible stems had sprung up around the sloop.

Imagine such an air-stalked dimple magnified so that the saucer was not a palm's breadth but a good spearcast across and the rodlike sword-straight stalk not a fingernail's width but a good four feet; imagine the sloop slid prow-foremost down into that shallow depression but stopping just short of the center and floating motionless there; imagine the bowsprit of the slightly tilted ship projecting over the exact center of the central tube or well of air; imagine a small, stalwart, nutbrown man in a gray loincloth lying along the bowsprit, his feet braced against the foredeck rails, and looking straight down the tube . . . and you have the Gray Mouser's situation exactly!

To be *in* the Mouser's situation and peering down the tube was very fascinating indeed, an experience calculated to drive other thoughts out of any man's mind— or even any woman's! The water here, a bowshot from the creamy rock-wall, was green, remarkably clear, but too deep to allow a view of the bottom—soundings taken yesterday had shown it to vary between six score and seven score feet. Through this water the well-size tube went down as perfectly circular and as smooth as if it were walled with glass; and indeed the Mouser would have believed that it was so walled—that the water immediately around it had been somehow frozen or hardened without altering in transparency—except that at the slightest noise, such as the Mouser's coughing, little quiverings would run up and down it in the form of series of ring-shaped waves.

What power prevented the tremendous weight of the sea from collapsing the tube in an instant, the Mouser could not begin to imagine.

Yet it was endlessly fascinating to peer down it. Sunlight transmitted through the sea water illuminated it to a considerable depth brightly if greenishly, and the circular wall played odd tricks with distance. For instance, at this moment the Mouser, peering down slantwise through the side of the tube, saw a thick fish as long as his arm swimming around it and nosing up to it. The shape of the fish was very familiar yet he could not at once name it. Then, thrusting his head out to one side and peering down at the same fish through the clear water alongside the tube, he saw that the fish was three times the length of his body—in fact, a shark. The Mouser shivered and told himself that the curved wall of the tube must act like the reduction lenses used by a few artists in Lankhmar.

On the whole, though, the Mouser might well have decided in the end that the vertical tunnel in the water was an illusion born of sun-glare and suggestion and have put on the ice-goggles and stuffed his ears with wax against any more siren-singing and then perhaps swigged at the forbidden brandy and gone to sleep, except for certain other circumstances footing the whole affair much more firmly in reality. For instance, there was a knotted rope securely tied to the bowsprit and hanging down the center of the tube, and this rope creaked from time to time with the weight on it, and also there were threads of black smoke coming out of the watery hole (these were what made the Mouser cough), and last but not least there was a torch burning redly far down in the hole— so far down its flame looked no bigger than a candle's —and just beside the flame, somewhat obscured by its

17

smoke and much tinied by distance, was the upward-peering face of Fafhrd!

The Mouser was inclined to take on faith the reality of anything Fafhrd got mixed up with, certainly anything that Fafhrd got physically into—the near-seven-foot Northerner was much too huge a hulk of solid matter to be picturable as strolling arm-in-arm with illusions.

The events leading up to the reality-footing facts of the rope, the smoke, and Fafhrd down the air-well had been quite simple. At dawn the sloop had begun to drift myste-riously among the water dimples, there being no percep-tible wind or current. Shortly afterwards it had bumped over the lip of the large saucer-shaped depression and slid to its present position with a little rush and then frozen there, as though the sloop's bowsprit and the hole were mutually desirous magnetic poles coupling together. Thereafter, while the Mouser had watched with eyes goggling and teeth a-chatter, Fafhrd had sighted down the hole, grunted with stolid satisfaction, slung the knotted rope down it, and then proceeded to array him-self, seemingly with both war and love in mind—pomad-ing his hair and beard, perfuming his hairy chest and armpits, putting on a blue silk tunic under the gleaming one of otterskin and all his silver-plated necklaces, arm-bands, brooches and rings as well, but also strapping longsword and axe to his sides and lacing on his spiked boots. Then he had lit a long thin torch of resinous pine in the gallery firebox, and when it was flaming bravely he had, despite the Mouser's solicitous cries and tugging protests, gone out on the bowsprit and lowered himself into the hole, using thumb and forefinger of his right hand to grip the torch and the other three fingers of that hand, along with his left hand, to grip the rope. Only then had he spoken, calling on the Mouser to make ready and follow him if the Mouser were more hot-blooded man than cold-blooded lizard.

The Mouser had made ready to the extent of stripping off most of his clothing—it had occurred to him it would be necessary to dive for Fafhrd when the hole became aware of its own impossibility and collapsed—and he had fetched to the foredeck his own sword Scalpel and dagger Cat's Claw in their case of oiled sealskin with the notion they might be needed against sharks. Thereafter he had simply poised on the bowsprit, as we have seen, observing Fafhrd's slow descent and letting the fascination of it all take hold of him.

At last he dipped his head and called softly down the hole, "Fafhrd, have you reached bottom yet?" frowning at the ring-shaped ripples even this gentle calling sent traveling down the hole and up again by reflection.

"WHAT DID YOU SAY?"

Fafhrd's answering bellow, concentrated by the tube and coming out of it like a solid projectile, almost blasted the Mouser off the bowsprit. Far more terrifying, the ring-ripples accompanying the bellow were so huge they almost seemed to close off the tube—narrowing it from four to two or three feet at any rate and dashing a spray of drops up into the Mouser's face as they reached the surface, lifting the rim upward as if the water were elastic, and then were reflected down the tube again.

The Mouser closed his eyes in a wince of horror, but when he opened them the hole was still there and the giant ring-ripples were beginning to abate.

Only a shade more loudly than the first time, but much more poignantly, the Mouser called down, "Fafhrd, don't do that again!"

"WHAT?"

This time the Mouser was prepared for it—just the same it was most horrid to watch those huge rings traveling up and down the tube in an arrow-swift green peristalsis. He firmly resolved to do no more calling, but just then Fafhrd started to speak up the tube in a voice of more rational volume—the rings produced were hardly thicker than a man's wrist.

"*Come on, Mouser! It's easy! You only have to drop the last six feet!*"

"Don't drop it, Fafhrd!" the Mouser instantly replied. "Climb back up!"

"*I already have! Dropped, I mean. I'm on the bottom. Oh, Mouser . . . !*"

The last part of Fafhrd's call was in a voice so infused with a mingled awe and excitement that the Mouser immediately asked back down, "What? 'Oh, Mouser'—what?"

"It's wonderful, it's amazing, it's fantastic!" the reply came back from below—this time very faintly all of a sudden, as if Fafhrd had somehow gone around an impossible bend or two in the tube.

"*What* is, Fafhrd?" the Mouser demanded—and this time his own voice raised moderate rings. "Don't go away, Fafhrd. But what *is* down there?"

"*Everything!*" the answer came back, not quite so faint this time.

"Are there girls?" the Mouser queried.

"*A whole world!*"

The Mouser sighed. The moment had come, he knew, as it always did, when outward circumstances and inner urges commanded an act, when curiosity and fascination tipped the scale of caution, when the lure of a vision and an adventure became so great and deep-hooking that he must respond to it or have his inmost self-respect eaten away.

Besides, he knew from long experience that the only way to extricate Fafhrd from the predicaments into which he got himself was to go fetch the perfumed and be-sworded lout!

So the Mouser sprang up lightly, clipped to his under-belt his sealskin-cased weapons, hung beside them in loops

20

a short length of knotted line with a slip-noose tied in one end, made sure that the sloop's hatches were securely covered and even that the galley fire was tightly boxed, rattled off a short scornful prayer to the Gods of Lankhmar, and lowered himself off the bowsprit and down into the green hole.

The hole was chilly and it smelt of fish, smoke, and Fafhrd's pomade. The Mouser's main concern as soon as he got in it, he discovered to his surprise, was not to touch its glassy sides. He had the feeling that if he so much as lightly brushed it, the water's miraculous "skin" would rupture and he would be engulfed—rather as an oiled needle floating on a bowl of water in its tiny hammock of "water skin" is engulfed and sinks when one pinks it. He descended rapidly knot by knot, supporting himself by his hands, barely touching his toes to the rope below, praying there would be no sway and that he would be able to check it if it started. It occurred to him he should have told Fafhrd to guy the rope at the bottom if he possibly could and above all have warned him not to shout up the tube while the Mouser descended—the thought of being squeezed by those dread water-rings was almost too much to bear. Too late now!—any word now would only too surely bring a bellow from the Northerner in reply.

First fears having been thus inspected though by no means banished, the Mouser began to take some note of his surroundings. The luminous green world was not just one emerald blank as it had seemed at first. There was life in it, though not in the greatest abundance: thin strands of scalloped maroon seaweed, near-invisible jellyfish trailing their opalescent fringes, tiny dark skates hovering like bats, small silvery backboned fish gliding and darting—some of them, a blue-and-yellow-ringed and black-spotted school, even contesting lazily over the *Black Treasurer*'s morning garbage, which the Mouser

21

recognized by a large pallid beef-bone Fafhrd had gnawed briefly before tossing overside.

Looking up, he was hard put not to gasp in horror. The hull of the sloop, pressing down darkly though pearled with bubbles, looked seven times higher above him than the distance he had descended by his count of the knots. Looking straight up the tube, however, he saw that the circle of deep blue sky had not shrunk correspondingly while the bowsprit bisecting it was still reassuringly thick. The curve of the tube had shrunk the sloop as it had the shark. The illusion was most weird and foreboding, nonetheless.

And now as the Mouser continued his swift descent, the circle overhead did grow smaller and more deeply blue, becoming a cobalt platter, a peacock saucer, and finally no more than a strange ultramarine coin that was the converging point of the tube and rope and in which the Mouser thought he saw a star flash. The Gray One puffed a few rapid kisses toward it, thinking how like they were to a drowning man's last bubbles. The light dimmed. The colors around him faded, the maroon seaweed turned gray, the fish lost their yellow rings, and the Mouser's own hands became blue as those of a corpse. And now he began to make out dimly the sea bottom, at the same extravagant distance below as the sloop was above, though immediately under him the bottom was oddly veiled or blanketed and only far off could he make out rocks and ridged stretches of sand.

His arms and shoulders ached. His palms burned. A monstrously fat grouper swam up to the tube and followed him down it, circling. The Mouser glared at it menacingly and it turned on its side and opened an impossibly large moon-crescent of mouth. The Mouser saw the razor teeth and realized it was the shark he'd seen or another like it, tinied by the lens of the tube. The teeth clashed, some of them inside the tube, only inches from his side. The water's "skin" did not rupture disastrously, although the Mouser got the eerie impression that the "bite" was bleeding a little water into the tube. The shark swam off to continue its circling at a moderate distance and the Mouser refrained from any more menacing looks.

Meanwhile the fishy smell had grown stronger and the smoke must have been getting thicker too, for now the Mouser coughed in spite of himself, setting the water-rings shooting up and down. He fought to suppress an anguished curse—and at that moment his toes no longer touched rope. He unloosed the extra coil from his belt, went down three more knots, tightened the slip-noose above the second knot from the bottom, and continued on his way.

Five handholds later his feet found a footing in cold muck. He gratefully unclenched his hands, working his cramped fingers, at the same time calling "Fafhrd!" softly but angrily. Then he looked around.

He was standing in the center of a large low tent of air, which was floored by the velvety sea-muck in which he had sunk to his ankles and roofed by the leadenly gleaming undersurface of the water—not evenly though, but in swells and hollows with ominous downward bulges here and there. The air-tent was about ten feet high at the foot of the tube. Its diameter seemed at least twenty times that, though exactly how far the edges extended it was impossible to judge for several reasons: the great irregularity of the tent's roof, the difficulty of even guessing at the extent of some outer areas where the distance between water-roof and muck-floor was measurable in inches, the fact that the gray light transmitted from above hardly permitted decent vision for more than two dozen yards, and finally the circumstance that there was considerable

23

torch-smoke in the way here and there, writhing in thick coils along the ceiling, collecting in topsy-turvey pockets, though eventually gliding sluggishly up the tube.

What fabulous invisible "tent-poles" propped up the oceans-heavy roof the Mouser could no more conceive than the force that kept the tube open.

Writhing his nostrils distastefully, both at the smoke and the augmented fishy smell, the Mouser squinted fiercely around the tent's full circumference. Eventually he saw a dull red glow in the black smudge where it was thickest, and a little later Fafhrd emerged. The reeking flame of the pine torch, which was still no more than half consumed, showed the Northerner bemired with sea-muck to his thighs and hugging gently to his side with his bent left arm a dripping mess of variously gleaming objects. He was stooped over somewhat, for the roof bulged down where he stood.

"Blubber brain!" the Mouser greeted him. "Put out that torch before we smother! We can see better without it. Oh oaf, to blind yourself with smoke for the sake of light!"

To the Mouser there was obviously only one sane way to extinguish the torch—jab it in the wet muck underfoot—but Fafhrd, though evidently most agreeable to the Mouser's suggestion in a vacantly smiling way, had another idea. Despite the Mouser's anguished cry of warning, he casually thrust the flaming stick into the watery roof.

There was a loud hissing and a large downward puff of steam, and for a moment the Mouser thought his worst dreads had been realized, for an angry squirt of water from the quenching point struck Fafhrd in the neck. But when the steam cleared it became evident that the rest of the sea was not going to follow the squirt, at least not at once; though now there was an ominous lump, like a

24

rounded tumor, in the roof where Fafhrd had thrust the torch, and from it water ran steadily in a stream thick as a quill, digging a tiny crater where it struck the muck below.

"Don't do that!" the Mouser commanded in unwise fury.

"This?" Fafhrd asked gently, poking a finger through the ceiling next to the dripping bulge. Again came the angry squirt, diminishing at once to a trickle, and now there were two bulges closely side by side, quite like breasts.

"Yes, *that*—not again," the Mouser managed to reply, his voice distant and high because of the self-control it took him not to rage at Fafhrd and so perhaps provoke even more reckless probings.

"Very well, I won't," the Northerner assured him. "Though," he added, gazing thoughtfully at the twin streams, "it would take those dribblings years to fill up this cavity."

"Who speaks of years down here?" the Mouser snarled at him. "Dolt! Iron Skull! What made you lie to me? 'Everything' was down here, you said—'a whole world.' And what do I find? Nothing! A miserable little cramp-roofed field of stinking mud!" And the Mouser stamped a foot in rage, which only splashed him foully, while a puffed, phosphorescent-whiskered fish expiring on the mire looked up at him reproachfully.

"That rude treading," Fafhrd said softly, "may have burst the silver-filigreed skull of a princess. 'Nothing,' say you? Look you then, Mouser, what treasure I have digged from your stinking field."

And as he came toward the Mouser, his big feet gliding gently through the top of the muck for all the spikes on his boots, he gently rocked the gleaming things cradled in his left arm and let the fingers of his right hand drift gently among them.

"Aye," he said, "jewels and gauds undreamed by those who sail above, yet all teased by me from the ooze while I sought another thing."

"What other thing, Gristle Dome?" the Mouser demanded harshly, though eyeing the gleaming things hungrily.

"The path," Fafhrd said a little querulously, as if the Mouser must know what he meant. "The path that leads from some corner or fold of this tent of air to the sea king's girls. These things are a sure promise of it. Look you, here, Mouser." And he opened his bent left arm a little and lifted out most delicately with thumb and fingertips a life-size metallic mask.

Impossible to tell in that drained gray light whether the metal were gold or silver or tin or even bronze and whether the wide wavy streaks down it, like the tracks of blue-green sweat and tears, were verdigris or slime. Yet it was clear that it was female, patrician, all-knowing yet alluring, loving yet cruel, hauntingly beautiful. The Mouser snatched it eagerly yet angrily and the whole lower face crumpled in his hand, leaving only the proud forehead and the eyeholes staring at him more tragically than eyes.

The Mouser flinched back, expecting Fafhrd to strike him, but in the same instant he saw the Northerner turning away and lifting his straight right arm, index finger a-point, like a slow semaphor.

"You were right, oh Mouser!" Fafhrd cried joyously. "Not only my torch's smoke but its very light blinded me. See! See the path!"

The Mouser's gaze followed Fafhrd's pointing. Now that the smoke was somewhat abated and the torch-flame no longer shot out its orange rays, the patchy phosphorescence of the muck and of the dying sea-things scattered about had become clearly visible despite the muted light filtering from above.

The phosphorescence was not altogether patchy, however. Beginning at the hole from which the knotted rope hung, a path of unbroken greenish-yellow witch-fire a long stride in width led across the muck toward an unpromising-looking corner of the tent of air where it seemed to disappear.

"Don't follow it, Fafhrd," the Mouser automatically enjoined, but the Northerner was already moving past him, taking long dreamlike strides. By degrees his cradling arm unbent and one by one his ooze-won treasures began to slip from it into the muck. He reached the path and started along it, placing his spike-soled feet in the very center.

"Don't follow it, Fafhrd," the Mouser repeated—a little hopelessly, almost whiningly, it must be admitted. "Don't follow it, I say. It leads only to squidgy death. We can still go back up the rope, aye, and take your loot with us . . ."

But meanwhile he himself was following Fafhrd and snatching up, though more cautiously than he had the mask, the objects his comrade let slip. It was not worth the effort, the Mouser told himself as he continued to do it: though they gleamed enticingly, the various necklaces, tiaras, filigreed breast-cups and great-pinned brooches weighed no more and were no thicker than plaitings of dead ferns. He could not seem to equal Fafhrd's delicacy and they fell apart at his touch.

Fafhrd turned back to him a face radiant as one who dreams sleeping of ultimate ecstasies. As the last ghost-gaud slipped from his arm, he said, "They are nothing—no more than the mask—mere sea-gnawed wraiths of treasure. But oh, the promise of them, Mouser! Oh, the promise!"

And with that he turned forward again and stooped under a large downward bulge in the low leaden-hued roof.

The Mouser took one look back along the glowing path to the small circular patch of sky-light with the knotted rope falling in the center of it. The twin streams of water coming from the two "wounds" in the ceiling seemed to be running more strongly—where they hit, the muck was splashing. Then he followed Fafhrd.

On the other side of the bulge the ceiling rose again to more than head-height, but the walls of the tent narrowed in sharply. Soon they were treading along a veritable tunnel in the water, a leaden arch-roofed passageway no wider than the phosphorescently yellow-green path that floored it. The tunnel curved just enough now to left, now to right, so that there was no seeing any long distance ahead. From time to time the Mouser thought he heard faint whistlings and moanings echoing along it. He stepped over a large crab that was backing feebly and saw beside it a dead man's hand emerging from the glowing muck, one shred-fleshed finger pointing the way they were taking.

Fafhrd half turned his head and muttered gravely, "Mark me, Mouser, there's magic in this somewhere!"

The Mouser thought he had never in his life heard a less necessary remark. He felt considerably depressed. He had long given up his puerile pleadings with Fafhrd to turn back—he knew there was no way of stopping Fafhrd short of grappling with him, and a tussle that would invariably send them crashing through one of the watery walls of the tunnel was by no means to his liking. Of course, he could always turn back alone. Still . . .

With the monotony of the tunnel and of just putting one foot after the other into the clinging muck and withdrawing it with a soft *plop*, the Mouser found time to

28

become oppressed, too, with the thought of the weight of the water overhead. It was as though he walked with all the ships of the world on his back. His imagination would picture nothing but the tunnel's instant collapse. He hunched his head into his shoulders, and it was all he could do not to drop to his elbows and knees and then stretch himself face down in the muck with the mere anticipation of the event.

The sea seemed to grow a little whiter ahead and the Mouser realized the tunnel was approaching the under-reaches of the curtain-wall of creamy rock he and Fafhrd had climbed yesterday. The memory of that climb let his imagination escape at last, perhaps because it fitted with the urge that he and Fafhrd somehow lift themselves out of their present predicament.

It had been a difficult ascent, although the pale rock had proved hard and reliable, for footholds and ledges had been few and they had had to rope up and go by way of a branching chimney, often driving pitons into cracks to create a support where none was—but they had had high hopes of finding fresh water and game, too, likely enough, so far west of Ool Hrusp and its hunters. At last they had reached the top, aching and a little blown from their climb and quite ready to throw themselves down and rest while they surveyed the landscape of grassland and stunted trees that they knew to be characteristic of other parts of this most lonely peninsula stretching south-westward between the Inner and Outer Seas.

Instead they had found . . . nothing. Worse than nothing, in a way, if that were possible. The longed-for top proved to be the merest edge of rock, three feet wide at the most and narrower some places, while on the other side the rock descended even more precipitously than on the side which they had climbed—indeed it was deeply undercut in large areas—and for an equal or rather some-

29

what greater distance. From the foot of this dizzying drop a wilderness of waves, foam and rocks extended to the horizon.

*They had found themselves clinging a-straddle to a veritable rock curtain, paper-thin in respect to its height and horizontal extent, between the Inner and what they realized must be the Outer Sea, which had eaten its way across the unexplored peninsula in this region but not yet quite broken through.* As far as eye could see in either direction the same situation obtained, though the Mouser fancied he could make out a thickening of the wall in the direction of Ool Hrusp.

Fafhrd had laughed at the surprise of the thing—gargantuan bellows of mirth that had made the Mouser curse him silently for fear the mere vibrations of his voice might shatter and tumble down the knife-edged saddle on which they perched. Indeed the Mouser had grown so angry with Fafhrd's laughter that he had sprung up and nimbly danced a jig of rage on the rock-ribbon, thinking meanwhile of wise Sheelba's saying: "Know it or not, man treads between twin abysses a tightrope that has neither beginning nor end."

Having thus expressed their feelings of horrified shock, each in his way, they had surveyed the yeasty sea below more rationally. The amount of surf and the numbers of emergent rocks showed it to be more shallow for some distance out—even likely, Fafhrd had opined, to drain itself at low tide, for his moon-lore told him that tides in this region of the world must at the moment be near high. Of the emergent rocks, one in particular stood out: a thick pillar two bowshots from the curtain-wall and as high as a four-story house. The pillar was spiraled by ledges that looked as if they were in part of human cutting, while set in its thicker base and emerging from the foam there appeared an oddly criss-crossed weed-fringed rectangle that looked mightily like a large stout door—though where such a door might lead and who would use it were perplexing questions indeed.

Then, since there was no answering that question or others and since there was clearly no fresh water or game to be had from this literal shell of a coast, they had descended back to the Inner Sea and the *Black Treasurer*, though now each time they had driven a piton it had been with the fear that the whole wall might split and collapse . . .

" 'Ware rocks!"

Fafhrd's warning cry pulled the Mouser out of his waking memory-dream—dropped him in a split instant as if it were, from the upper reaches of the creamy curtain-wall to a spot almost an equal distance below its sea-gnawed base. Just ahead of him three thick lumpy daggers of rock thrust down inexplicably through the gray watery ceiling of the tunnel. The Mouser shudderingly wove his head past them, as Fafhrd must have, and then looking beyond his comrade he saw more rocky protuberances encroaching on the tunnel from all sides—saw, in fact, as he strode on, that the tunnel was changing from one of water and muck to one roofed, walled and floored with solid rock. The water-borne light faded away behind them, but the increasing phosphorescence natural to the animal life of a sea cavern almost compensated for it, boldly outlining their wet stony way and here and there glowing with especial brilliance and variety of color from the bands, portholes, feelers and eye-rings of many a dying fish and crawler.

The Mouser realized they must be passing far under the curtain-wall he and Fafhrd had climbed yesterday and that the tunnel ahead must be leading under the Outer Sea they had seen tossing with billows. There was no longer that immediate oppressive sense of a crushing weight of ocean overhead or of brushing elbows with magic. Yet the thought that if the tube, tent and tunnel

31

behind them should collapse, then a great gush of solid water would rush into the rock-tunnel and engulf them, was in some ways even worse. Back under the water roof he'd had the feeling that even if it should collapse he might reach the surface alive by bold swimming and conceivably drag the cumbered Fafhrd up with him. But here they'd be hopelessly trapped.

True, the tunnel seemed to be ascending, but not enough or swiftly enough to please the Mouser. Moreover, if it did finally emerge, it would be to that shattering welter of foam they'd peered down at yesterday. Truly, the Mouser found it hard to pick between his druthers, or even to have any druthers at all. His feelings of depression and doom gradually sank to a new and perhaps ultimate nadir, and in a desperate effort to wrench them up he deliberately imagined to himself the zestiest tavern he knew in Lankhmar—a great gray cellar all a-flare with torches, wine streaming and spilling, tankards and coins a-clink, voices braying and roaring, poppy fumes a-twirl, naked girls writhing in lascivious dances . . .

"Oh, Mouser . . . !"

Fafhrd's deep and feelingful whisper and the Northerner's large hand against his chest halted the Mouser's plodding, but whether it fetched his spirit back below the Outer Sea or simply produced a fantastic alteration in its escapist imagining, the Gray One could not at once be sure.

They were standing in the entrance to a vast submarine grotto that rose in multiple steps and terraces toward an indefinite ceiling from which cascaded down like silver mist a glow about thrice the strength of moonlight. The grotto reeked of the sea like the tunnel behind them; it was likewise scattered with expiring fish and eels and small octopuses; molluscs tiny and huge clustered on its

32

walls and corners between weedy draperies and silver-green veils; while its various niches and dark circular doorways and even the stepped and terraced floor seemed shaped in part at least by the action of rushing waters and grinding sand.

The silver mist did not fall evenly but concentrated itself in swirls and waves of light on three terraces. The first of these was placed centrally, and only a level stretch and then a few low ledges separated it from the tunnel's mouth. Upon this terrace was set a great stone table with weed-fringed sides and mollusc-crusted legs but level top of grained and spotted marble polished to what looked an exquisite smoothness. A great golden basin stood on one end of this table and two golden goblets beside the basin.

Beyond the first terrace rose a second uneven flight of steps with areas of menacing shadow pressing upon it from either side. Behind the areas of darkness were a second and third terrace that the silvery light favored. The one on the right—Fafhrd's side, to call it that, for he stood to the right in the tunnel mouth—was walled and arched with mother-of-pearl, almost as if it were one gigantic shell, and pearly swells rose from its floor like heaped satin pillows. The one on the Mouser's side, slightly below, was backed by an arras of maroon sea-weed that fell in wide scalloped strands and billowed on the floor. From between these twin terraces the flight of irregular steps or ledges continued upward into a third area of darkness.

Shifting shadows and dark wavings and odd gleamings hinted that the three areas of darkness might be occupied; there was no doubt that the three bright terraces were. On the upper terrace on Fafhrd's side stood a tall and opulently beautiful woman whose golden hair rose in spiral masses like a shell and whose dress of golden fishnet

33

clung to her pale greenish flesh. Her fingers showed greenish webs between them and on the side of her neck as she turned were faint scorings like a fish's gills.

On the Mouser's side was a slimmer yet exquisitely feminine creature whose silver flesh seemed to merge into silver scales on shoulders, back and flanks under her robe of filmy violet and whose short dark hair was split back from her low forehead's center by a scalloped silver crest a hand's breadth high. She too showed the faint neck-scorings and finger webs.

The third figure, standing a-crouch behind the table, was sexlessly scrawny, with an effect of wiry old age, and either gowned or clad closely in jet black. A shock of rope-thick hair dark red as iron rust covered her head while her gills and finger webs were starkly apparent.

Each of these women wore a metal mask resembling in form and expression the eaten-away one Fafhrd had found in the muck. That of the first figure was gold; of the second, silver; of the third, green-splotched sea-darkened bronze.

The first two women were still, not as if they were part of a show but as though they were observing one. The scrawny black sea-witch was vibrantly active, although she hardly moved on her black-webbed toes except to shift position abruptly and ever so slightly now and then. She held a short whip in either hand, the webs folded outside her bent knuckles, and with these whips she maintained and directed the swift spinning of a half dozen objects on the polished table top. What these objects were it was impossible to say, except that they were roughly oval. Some by their semi-transparency as they spun might have been large rings or saucers, others actual tops by their opacity. They gleamed silver and green and golden and they spun so swiftly and moved in such swift intersecting orbits as they spun that they seemed to leave gleaming wakes of spin in the misty air

34

behind them. Whenever one would flag in its spinning and its true form begin to blink into visibility, she'd bring it back up to speed again with two or three rapid whip-flips; or should one veer too close to the table's edge or the golden basin, or threaten to collide with another, she'd redirect its orbit with deft lashings; now and again, with incredible skill, she'd flick one so that it jumped high in the air and then flick it again at landing so that it went on spinning without a break, leaving above it an evanescent loop of silvery air-spin.

These whirring objects made the pulsing moans and whistles the Mouser had heard along the tunnel.

As he watched them now and listened to them, the Gray One became convinced—partly because the silvery cruving tubes of spin made him think of the air shaft he'd rope-climbed and the air-tunnel he'd plodded—that these spinning things were a crucial part of the magic that had created and held open the path through the Inner Sea behind them, and that once they should cease whirring then the shaft and tent and tunnel would collapse and the waters of the Inner Sea speed through the rock-tunnel into this grotto.

And indeed the scrawny black sea-witch looked to the Mouser as though she'd been whipping her tops for hours and—more to the point—would be able to keep on whipping them for hours more. She showed no signs of her exertion save the rhythmic rise and fall of her breastless chest and the extra whistle of breath through the mouth-slit of her mask and the gape and close of her gills.

Now she seemed for the first time to see him and Fafhrd, for without leaving off her whipping she thrust her bronze mask toward them, red ropes a-spill across its green-blotched forehead, and glared at them—hungrily, it seemed. Yet she made them no other menace, but after a searching scrutiny jerked back her head twice, as if for a sign that they should go past her. At the same

35

time the green and silver queens beckoned to them languorously.

This woke the Mouser and Fafhrd from their dazed watching and they complied eagerly enough, though in passing the table the Mouser sniffed wine and paused to take up the two golden goblets, handing one to his comrade. They drained them despite the green hue of the drink, for the stuff smelt right and was fiery sweet yet tart.

As he drank, the Mouser saw into the golden bowl. It held no store of green wine, but was filled almost to the brim with a crystal fluid that might or might not have been water. On the fluid floated a model, hardly a finger long, of the hull of a black boat. A tiny tube of air seemed to go down from its prow.

But there was no time for closer looking, for Fafhrd was moving on. The Mouser stepped up into his area of shadow to the left as Fafhrd had done to the right . . . and as he so stepped, there sidled from the shadows before him two bluely pallid men armed each with a pair of wave-edged knives. They were sailors, he judged from their pigtails and shuffling gait, although they were both naked, and they were indisputably dead—by token of their unhealthy color, their carelessness of the thick slime streaking them, the way their bulging eyes showed only whites and the bottom crescent of the irises, and the fact that their hair, ears, and other portions of their anatomies looked somewhat fish-chewed. Behind them waddled a scimitar-wielding dwarf with short spindle legs and monstrous head and gills—a veritable walking embryo. His great saucer eyes too were the upturned ones of a dead thing, which did not make the Mouser feel any easier as he whisked Scalpel and Cat's Claw out of their sealskin case, for the three converged on him confidently

36

where he stood and rapidly shifted to block his way as he sought to circle behind them.

It was probably just as well that the Mouser had at that moment no attention to spare for his comrade's predicament. Fafhrd's area of shadow was black as ink toward the wall, and as the Northerner strode through the margin of it past a ridged and man-sized knob of rock rising from the ledges and between him and the Mouser, there lifted from the further blackness—like eight giant serpents rearing from their lair—the thick, sinuous, crater-studded arms of a monstrous octopus. The sea-beast's movement must have struck internal sparks, for it simultaneously flashed into a yellow-streaked purplish iridescence, showing Fafhrd its baleful eyes large as plates, its cruel beak big as the prow of an overturned skiff, and the rather unlikely circumstance that the end of each mighty tentacle wrapped powerfully around the hilt of a gleaming broadsword.

Snatching at his own sword and axe, Fafhrd backed away from the be-weaponed squid against the ridged knob of rock. Two of the ridges, being the vertical shell-edges of a mollusc four feet across, instantly closed on the slack of his otterskin tunic, firmly holding him there.

Greatly daunted but determined to live nevertheless, the Northerner swung his sword in a great figure eight, the lower loop of which almost nicked the floor, while the upper loop rose above his head like a tall arching shield. This double-petalled flower of steel baffled the four blades or so with which the octopus first came chopping at him rather cautiously, and as the sea monster drew back his arms for another volley of slashes, Fafhrd's left arm licked out with his axe and chopped through the nearest tentacle.

His adversary hooted loudly then and struck repeatedly with all his swords, and for a space it looked as though

37

Fafhrd's universal parry must surely be pierced, but then the axe licked out again from the center of the sword-shield, once, twice, and two more tentacle tips fell and the swords they gripped with them. The octopus drew back then out of reach and sprayed a great mist-cloud of stinking black ink from its tube, under cover of which it might work its will unseen on the pinned North-erner, but even as the blinding mist billowed toward him Fafhrd hurled his axe at the huge central head. And al-though the black fog hid the axe almost as soon as it left his hand, the heavy weapon must have reached a vital spot, for immediately the octopus hurled its remaining swords about the grotto at random (fortunately striking no one although they made a fine clatter) as its tentacles thrashed in dying convulsions.

Fafhrd drew a small knife, slashed his otterskin tunic down the front and across the shoulders, stepped out of it with a contemptuous wave to the mollusc as if to say, "Have it for supper if you will," and turned to see how his comrade fared. The Mouser, bleeding greenly from two trivial wounds in ribs and shoulder, had just finished severing the major tendons of his three hideous oppo-nents—this having proved the only way to immobilize them when various mortal wounds had slowed them in no way at all nor caused them to bleed one drop of blood of any color.

He smiled sickishly at Fafhrd and turned with him to-ward the upper terraces. And now it became clear that the Green and Silver Ones were at least in one respect true queens, for they had not fled the prodigious battles as lesser women might, but abided them and now waited with arms lightly outstretched. Their gold and silver masks could not smile, but their bodies did, and as the two adventurers mounted toward them from the shadow into the light (the Mouser's little wounds changing from green to red, but Fafhrd's blue tunic staying pretty inky) it seemed to them that veily finger-webs and light neck-scorings were the highest points of female beauty. The lights faded somewhat on the upper terraces, though not on the lower where the monotonous six-toned music of the tops kept reassuringly on, and the two heroes entered each into that dark lustrous realm where all thoughts of wounds are forgotten and all memories of even the zestiest Lankhmar wine-cellar grow flat, and the Sea, our cruel mother and loving mistress, repays all debts.

A great soundless jar, as of the rock-solid earth moving, recalled the Mouser to his surroundings. Almost simultaneously the whir of one of the tops mounted to a high-pitched whine ending in a tinkly crash. The silver light began to pulse and flicker wildly throughout the grotto. Springing to his feet and looking down the steps, the Mouser saw a memory-etching sight: the rust-topped black sea witch whipping wildly at her rebellious tops, which leaped and bounded about the table like fierce silver weasels, while through the air around her from all sides but chiefly from the tunnel there converged an arrow-swift flight of flying fish, skates, and ribbon-edged eels, all inky black and with tiny jaws agape.

At that instant Fafhrd seized him by the shoulder and jerked him fully around, pointing up the ledges. A silver lightning-flash showed a great cross-beamed, weed-fringed door at the head of the rocky stairs. The Mouser nodded violently—meaning he understood it resembled and must be the door they had yesterday seen from the ribbony cliff-summit—and Fafhrd, satisfied his comrade would follow him, dashed toward it up the ledges.

But the Mouser had a different thought and darted in the opposite direction in the face of an ominous wet reeking wind. Returning a dozen lightning-flashes later, he saw the green and silver queens disappearing into round black tunnel mouths in the rock to either side of the terrace and then they were gone.

39

As he joined Fafhrd in the work of unsettling the cross-bars of the great weedy door and drawing its massive rusty bolts, it quivered under a portentous triple knocking as though someone had smote it thrice with a long-skirted cloak of chain mail. Water squirted under it and through the lower third of the central vertical crack. The Mouser looked behind him then, with the thought that they might yet have to seek another avenue of escape . . . and saw a great white-headed pillar of water jetting more than half the height of the grotto from the mouth of the tunnel connecting with the Inner Sea. Just then the silver cavern-light went out, but almost immediately other light spilled from above. Fafhrd had heaved open half of the great door. Green water foamed about their knees and subsided. They fought their way through and as the great door slammed behind them under a fresh surge of water, they found themselves sloshing about on a wild beach blown with foam, swimming with surf, and floored chiefly with large flat water-worn oval rocks like giants' skipping stones. The Mouser, turned shoreward, squinted desperately at the creamy cliff two bowshot away, wondering if they could possibly reach it through the mounting tide and climb it if they did.

But Fafhrd was looking seaward. The Mouser again felt himself shoulder-grabbed, spun around, and this time dragged up a curving ledge of the great tower-rock in the base of which was set the door through which they had just emerged. He stumbled, cutting his knees, but was jerked ruthlessly on. He decided that Fafhrd must have some very good reason for so rudely enjoining haste and thereafter did his best to hurry without assistance at Fafhrd's heels up the spiraling ramplike ledge. On the second circling he stole a seaward look, gasped, and increased the speed of his mad dizzy scramble.

The stony beach below was drained and only here and

there patched with huge gouts of spume, but roaring toward them from outer ocean was a giant wave that looked almost half as high as the pillar they were mounting—a great white wall of water flecked with green and brown and studded with rocks—a wave such as distant earthquakes send charging across the sea like a massed cavalry of monsters. Behind that wave came a taller one, and behind that a third taller still.

The Mouser and Fafhrd were three gasping circles higher when the stout tower shuddered and shook to the crashing impact of the first giant wave. Simultaneously the landward door at its base burst open from within and the cavern-traveling water from the Inner Sea gushed out creamily to be instantly engulfed. The crest of the wave caught at Fafhrd's and the Mouser's ankles without quite tripping them or much slowing their progress. The second and third did likewise, although they had gained another circle before each impact. There was a fourth wave and a fifth, but no higher than the third. The two adventurers reached the stumpy summit and cast themselves down on it, clutching at the still-shaking rock and slewing around to watch the shore—Fafhrd noting the astonishing minor circumstance that the Mouser was gripping between his teeth in the corner of his mouth a small black cigar.

The creamy curtain wall shuddered at the impact of the first wave and great cracks ran across it. The second wave shattered it and it fell into the third with an explosion of spray, displacing so much salt water that the return wave almost swamped the tower, its dirty crest tugging at the Mouser's and Fafhrd's fingers and licking along their sides. Again the tower shook and rocked beneath them but did not fall and that was the last of the great waves. Fafhrd and the Mouser circled down the spiraling ledges until they caught up with the declining

41

sea, which still deeply covered the door at the tower's base. Then they looked landward again, where the mist raised by the catastrophe was dissipating.

A full half mile of curtain-wall had collapsed from base to crest, its shards vanishing totally beneath the waves, and through that gap the higher waters of the Inner Sea were pouring in a flat sullen tide that was swiftly obliterating the choppy aftermath of the earthquake waves from the Outer Sea.

On this wide river in the sea the *Black Treasurer* appeared from the mist, riding straight toward their refuge rock.

Fafhrd cursed superstitiously. Sorcery working against him he could always accept, but magic operating in his favor he invariably found disturbing.

As the sloop drew near, they dove together into the sea, reached it with a few brisk strokes, scrambled aboard, steered it past the rock, and then lost no time in toweling and dressing their nakedness and preparing hot drink. Soon they were looking at each other over steaming mugs of grog.

"Now that we've changed oceans," Fafhrd said, "we'll raise No-ombrulsk in a day with this west wind."

The Mouser nodded and then smiled steadily at his comrade for a space. Finally he said, "Well, old friend, are you sure that is all you have to say?"

Fafhrd frowned. "Well, there's one thing," he replied somewhat uncomfortably after a bit. "Tell me, Mouser, did your girl ever take off her mask?"

"Did yours?" the Mouser asked back, eyeing him quizzically.

Fafhrd frowned. "Well, more to the point," he said gruffly, "did any of it really happen? We lost our swords and duds but we have nothing to show for it."

The Mouser grinned and took the black cigar from the corner of his mouth and handed it to Fafhrd.

42

"This is what I went back for," he said, sipping his grog. "I thought we needed it to get our ship back, and perhaps we did."

It was a tiny replica, carved in jet with the Mouser's teeth marks deeply indenting it near the stern, of the *Black Treasurer*.

As Suar-Peial of Amferé, "by trade a singer of sweet songs," draws his slim bronze rapier, he may perhaps remind you of François Villon, likewise a singer of sweet songs and a swordsman, and, as is Suar, a man of his time. The worlds of François Villon and Suar Peial have much in common.

# THE STRONGER SPELL

## by L. Sprague De Camp

# THE STRONGER SPELL

DIMLY seen through an autumnal drizzle that made the cobblestones of its waterfront glow in the fading light, the city of Kernê—ancient, bustling, colorful, and wicked —brooded over the waters of the Western Ocean. The flying-fish flags of the city stirred in sopping folds from poles atop the watchtowers along the walls, where sentries paced and peered through the murk.

Along broad Ocean Street, as the waterfront was called, few folk moved in the dusk and water gurgled in the gutters. Most of the tubby roundships that carried Kernê's commerce and the slender galleys that protected it from the corsairs of the Gorgon Isles had been laid up for the season, hauled out of water into sheds along the beach south of the waterfront proper. Hence few ships were using the quays and piers of Ocean Street except the usual scuttle of fishing craft, and most of these were sitting out the storm.

A two-horse chariot came pop-ploping by, its bronze tires banging harshly on the cobbles and its driver braced against the pull of the half-wild horses. The passenger was muffled to the eyes against the wet, but lights from the houses caught the golden trimmings of the vehicle and told that he must be one of the oligarchy of merchant princes.

Suar Peial, hugging a couple of bulky objects under his cloak, strode along the street, paying little heed to the questionable characters who peered out of doorways and alleys. These took in Suar's stature and the slender scabbard visible below the cloak, and looked elsewhere for easier pickings.

A noise from an alley attracted Suar's attention. A glance showed a fight in progress. A man with his back to an angle in the wall was defending himself by kicks and the blows of some sort of club against an attack by five others. The looks of these latter, as tattered as the falling leaves of the cork oaks that lined Kernê's avenues, told Suar that they were typical thieves of the quarter.

A sensible man on the Kernean waterfront would walk swiftly away, pretending that he had seen or heard nothing amiss. But if Suar had been sensible he would not have been in Kernê in the first place. He would have been home in Zhysk across the Sirenian Sea; he might even have been king of Zhysk. As it was, the lone man was due to go down under the clubs and swords of his attackers in a matter of a few heartbeats. Even had he been twice as big and much better armed, he could not face five ways at once. If his cowardly assailants had been willing to risk a hard knock or two in closing, they would already have had him down.

Suar shucked off the cloak, made a bundle of the cloak and the objects that he had been carrying, drew his slim bronze rapier, and started for the scene. As he went, he picked his first opponent—the one with the cudgel. Of the others, two carried short bronze broadswords and the remaining two, knives. With shield or armor, Suar would have had little to fear from the club, but lacking de-

48

fenses he feared to fence with it, lest a wild swing snap his thirty-inch blade.

The man with the club turned at the sound of Suar's approach and sprang back. The other four backed away from their victim also, their attitude bespeaking imminent flight. Then he of the club said, "There is but one. Slay him too!"

He stepped forward himself, swinging the bludgeon. Suar did not try to parry; instead, his long knobby arms and legs shot out in a lunge that sent his point through the club-man's arm. Suar bounced back, trying to recover before the club arrived. He did not quite succeed. Although the blow went weak and awry because of the wound in the thief's arm, the wood still grazed Suar's scalp, scraped his right ear, and bounced off his right shoulder—a painful knock, but not a disabling one. Then the club clattered to the ground as its owner's grip failed.

As the man stood there, holding his wounded arm and staring stupidly, Suar's sword flicked out again like a serpent's tongue and the point pierced the thief's broad chest. The club-man, coughing a curse, folded up into the mud of the alley. As the others began to close in upon Suar, the latter shot a thrust at the nearest swordsman, who gave ground, then engaged one of the knife-wielders. The man tried to grab the blade with his free hand, but Suar avoided the clutch and thrust him through the body.

All this had taken as much time as an unhurried man would require to breathe thrice. At that instant a sharp sound drew the glances of all. The original victim had stepped up behind his nearest assailant and brought the club-thing down upon the latter's head with a mighty blow.

Then there were three thieves lying in the mud and two others fleeing. One of those lying in the alley still moved and groaned.

Suar looked at the man whom he had rescued. He could not make out much in the dim light, save that the man wore the tartan trousers and the sweeping mustache of the northeasterly barbarians. The man stood back, gripping his club-thing as if still doubtful of Suar's intentions.

"You may put that away, fellow," said Suar, straightening his blade. "No robber am I, but a mere poetaster."

"Who are you then?" asked the shorter man. Like Suar he spoke the bastard Hesperian of the ports of the Western Ocean, but with a strange spitting accent.

"I am Suar Peial of Amferé, by trade a singer of sweet songs. And you, good sir?"

The man made some curious sounds in his throat, as if he were imitating the growl of a dog.

"What said you?" asked Suar.

"I said my name was Ghw Gleokh. I suppose I should thank you for rescuing me."

"Your eloquence overwhelms me. Are you a stranger?"

"That I am," said Ghw Gleokh. "Help me bind up these cuts." As Suar bandaged Ghw's two slight wounds the latter inquired, "Could you tell me where in Kernê one can buy a drop of wine wherewith to wash down one's bread?"

Suar said, "I was on my way to Derende's tavern to ply my trade. I have no objection to your coming along."

As he spoke, Suar wiped his blade on the clothing of the nearest corpse, sheathed it, and turned away. He picked up his cloak and the bundles wrapped therein and resumed his course. Ghw Gleokh trotted after him with the broadsword of the dead swordsman, for he had none of his own.

Suar walked steadily to Derende's tavern and shouldered his way around the leather curtain that served as a door. He had to duck to avoid hitting his head on the

50

top of the doorframe, for he came from Poseidonis across the western seas—or Pusad as it was called—where six and a half feet was not unusual stature. A central hearth-fire crackled and snapped, its glow picking out faces bearded and faces bare, and its smoke forming a blue pall that crept sluggishly out the hole in the roof. It was a small fire, for Kernê never got really cold.

Suar threaded his way among the crowded benches, nodded to a couple of acquaintances, and eased his bundles on to Derende's serving counter. One was a battered old lyre; the other a provision-bag of coarse sacking which smelled strongly of seafood, even above the many odors of the inn.

"Oh, it's the poet," said Derende, pushing his huge paunch up against the other side of the counter. "Well, vagabond?"

"Well indeed, mine host!" cried Suar. "I bring you, to cook for my supper, the very queen of sea-creatures; the pearl among fish. Behold!"

He loosened the draw-string of the provision-bag and dumped out upon the counter a very large octopus. Ghw, who had been crowding behind him to see, leaped back with a hoarse cry.

"Gods!" he cried. "That is the world's monster for fair! Are you sure it is dead?"

"Quite sure," said Suar, grinning.

"No doubt you stole it from some poor fisherman," growled Derende.

"How the world misjudges an artist!" said Suar. "If I told you I had gotten it honestly you wouldn't believe me, so why should I argue? In any case, cook it properly with olive-oil and a few greens, and serve it up with a skin of the best green wine of Zhysk."

Derende began to gather up the octopus. "The greens and the oil you may have in return for your croaking, but any wine you will have to pay for."

"Alas! I had some trade-metal earlier today, but I got into a game of knucklebones. If you would let me have credit until I have sung and passed my scrip. . . ."

Derende shook his head. "In that case Barley-beer will do for the likes of you."

"Lyr's barnacles!" exclaimed Suar. "How do you expect me to sing on that bilgewater?" He gestured towards the rest of the room. "You don't suppose all these people have crowded in here for love of your bitter beer and sour face, do you? They came to hear me. Who fills your stinking hovel night after night?"

"You heard me," said Derende. "Beer it shall be, or take your squawk elsewhere. I'll get in a girl; some bouncing bosomy wench who'll not only sing 'em but also—"

Ghw Gleokh stepped up and laid on the counter a small copper wedge, shaped like an axhead in minature and stamped with the flying-fish of Kernê.

"Here," he said in his weird accent. "Give us a sack of wine." Derende smiled at the coin.

"That is more the spirit," said Suar. "Master Derende, you old tub of lard, have you seen my friend Midawan the smith?"

"Not tonight," said Derende, lugging out a leather bottle and a couple of tarred leather drinking-jacks.

"He'll be in later, no doubt," said Suar. "What's news?"

Derende replied, "The Senate has hired a new wizard, a Tartessian named Barik."

"What happened to the old one?"

"They had him impaled because of that sandstorm."

"What is this?" asked Ghw with interest.

Derende explained. "He conjured up a sandstorm to overwhelm a camel-raid of desert-dwelling Lixitans, but by misdirection buried a score of our own warriors instead. What news have you, Suar?"

"Oh, young Okkozen, the son of Bulkajmi the Consul, was arrested for driving his chariot recklessly while drunk. Because of his connections, the magistrate let him off with an admonition. And Geddel the trader has been murdered in the Atlantean Mountains by a witch whom he tried to cheat out of her price for death-charms." Suar turned to his companion. "Good Ghw, let's find a seat, if we have to pitch one of these greasy Kerneans out on his rump. You shall share my beautiful octopus while I in return munch a piece of your bread."

"The bread you may have, because of my debt to you," said Ghw sourly, "but red-hot sword-blades would not force me to eat a piece of that hideous sea-monster.

"The bigger fool you." Suar, looking over the heads of the throng, pointed. "I see a bench as vacant as my purse. Come on."

The bench was one of two flanking a corner table. Two men occupied the bench opposite with their backs against the wall, black cloaks drawn up over their heads. At first, Suar took them for Euskerians because of the cloaks, but as he sat down he became aware of an inindefinable alienness about them. The younger and larger one, with the pimples, ate bread and cheese while the older and smaller did not eat, but inhaled the pungent smoke that rose from a tiny brazier on the table in front of him. They paid no attention to the new arrivals.

Suar rolled up his cloak and stuffed it under the bench, revealing that under it he wore the striped kilt of Poseidonis and an old shirt of what had been fine-grade wool, now much patched and mended. He pushed in to the wallward end of the bench, facing the small black-clad stranger, while Ghw likewise disposed of his cloak and took the other end. Suar poured out mugs of wine while Ghw went to work with his knife on the loaf of barley-bread he carried, now slightly soggy from the rain. Presently they were both munching and gulping.

Suar, his mouth full, asked, "My dear old comrade, what's that curious thing with which you were smiting the thieves, like Zormé belaboring the Bruthonians? It looks like nothing I ever saw."

Ghw, a short man with reddish hair and arms of simian length, gave his companion a blank stare. "That is something I do not discuss," he growled.

Suar shrugged. "Be a louse, then." He twanged the strings of his lyre and spoke to the small man across the table. "Your pardon, sir, but that smoke does not impress me as a very nourishing diet. If you would like a piece of the finest octopus salad in Kernê, I shall be pleased to spare you a portion when it arrives, for the monster is too large for even my ample capacity."

The man looked up at last, his pupils mere dots in the flickering glow of the rush-light that stood in a little bronze holder in the middle of the table. He said, "Your intentions are meritorious, for which you shall receive credit in the ledgers of the gods. But know, mortal, that when the soul is properly fed, the body takes care of itself."

"Mortal yourself," said Suar. "It appears, then, that I shall have to eat the whole thing—"

"Not so," said a new voice. "I have brought it over to share it with you."

A dark man of medium height and enormous brawn, with somewhat negroid hair and features, stood at the end of the table holding a great wooden platter on which was heaped up a pile of steaming pieces of cooked octopus. "Move that light, old giraffe, and change places with this red-haired one."

He slid the platter down the table, pulled up a stool,

and planked down a slab of cheese, a half-loaf of bread, and a bag of jujubes as his contribution to the meal.

"No," said Suar. "This red-haired one is my friend, by virtue of my having just saved his life." Suar gave a slightly inflated account of the battle in the alley, adding, "His name is Ghw Gleokh, if you will believe it. If you can't say it, just clear your throat and you will come close enough. I should guess he hails from one of the barbarous and bloody Keltic tribes. Is that right, Ghw?"

"All but the part about our being barbarians. I am a Galathan. Who is this man?"

"My old friend, Midawan the armorer," said Suar. "He eats bronze spearheads for breakfast, and comes from Tegrazen, to the south, which is on the borders of Blackland. Though of partly Black descent he swears he has never tasted human flesh. I twit him about it when he vexes me."

"Some day you will twit me once too often," said Midawan, sitting down on the stool at the end of the table, "and I'll tie that swan's neck of yours in a knot. Here, Galathan, have a tentacle!"

"Take that slimy sea-creature away!" said Ghw. "Is there no such thing as an honest roast in Kernê?"

"Certainly," said Suar, "for the rich. We common folk deem ourselves lucky to taste one on the Feast of Korb. It was not so in my homeland, where we gorged on bison steaks every day. And speaking of hunting, is that mysterious bronze bar of yours some sort of weapon or hunting-implement?"

Ghw Gleokh had now drunk enough wine to have mellowed. He belched loudly and said, "You might say so; you might say so. It is in fact a magical tool of the highest power. When properly used neither man nor beast can stand before it."

At this point the larger and younger of the cloaked

men across the table spoke. "Ha, hear the barbarian brag!"

Ghw stiffened. "Sir, I do not know you, but I do not let riffraff speak to me in that manner."

"As to that," said the cloaked one, "I am Qahura, apprentice magician, and this is my master, Semkaf. We come from the city of Typhon in the land of Setesh, whose magic is as far beyond yours as yours is beyond the mudpies of children."

"Quiet, fool," muttered the older magician, the one identified as Semkaf.

"But master, it is not meet that these savages should taunt and flout us. They must be taught a lesson."

"If there is any teaching to be done," said Ghw loudly, "I shall do it. I am an initiate druid of the Galatha, known to all, whereas I have never heard of your Typhon and doubt it exists."

Qahura said, "Indeed it exists, as you would learn soon enough did you visit us and were flayed upon our sacrificial altars. Typhon rises in black and purple from the mystic margins of the Sea of Thesh, amid the towering pyramidal tombs of kings who reigned in splendor over Setesh when mighty Torrutseish was but a village and golden Kernê but a vacant stretch of beach. No man living knows the full tale of Typhon's history, or the convolutions of its streets and secret passageways, or the hoarded treasure of its kings, or the hidden powers of its wizards. As for you," sneered the apprentice, "if you are a druid, where are your white robe and crown of mistletoe? What are you doing in Kernê?"

"Oh, that, my bombastic young friend, is a matter of tribal politics. Our arch-druid died suddenly and some were evil-minded enough to say I had stabbed him."

Qahura said, "His vaunted druidic magic was evidently not able to turn knife-blades. Can you do anything besides read the weather signs?"

"All that you can do, and much besides. For instance, would you see the heroes of the Galatha?"

Without awaiting an answer Ghw swept his hand back and forth across the table, muttering a spell. At once a score of little figures, about the size of a man's thumb, appeared on the table, some afoot, some mounted, and some in scythe-wheeled chariots. Some wore barbarian trews while others were naked and painted in bizarre patterns. They darted about, their cries sounding in Suar's ears like the buzzing of gnats. A couple began to fight, lunging and slashing with swords the size of splinters.

"Ha!" said Qahura. "Dainty little mannikins, but one of the sacred cats of Setesh would make short work of them."

He cast a spell in his turn, whereupon a large yellow cat appeared upon the table. It pounced on a miniature Galathan and began to worry it like a mouse. With a gesture Ghw swept the other heroes into nothingness, but the cat continued to bait its victim.

"All that you can do I can do, and better," said Ghw. "If you conjure up a familiar in the form of a cat, I will fetch one in that of a wolf, and we shall see—"

"Gentlemen!" said Suar, laying a hand on Ghw's arm. "Before this competition works up to lions and mammoths, consider that Derende's tavern is no place for fights between such creatures. They would squash us and the other customers like bugs in their struggles. Moreover I haven't yet sung my songs and passed my wallet. I urge that you wait until the weather clears and repair to an open field outside the walls, and then have at each other with your entire demonic retinues. The Kerneans would love the sport."

"There is something in what you say, poet," said Qahura. "Still, let it be understood that we of Setesh have the utmost contempt for any spells that this unfrocked

57

druid could bring into action. For my master Semkaf commands the great serpent Apepis itself, which could swallow Master Ghw and all his minions at one gulp."

"I fear it not," said Ghw, reaching under the bench. "Here is the strongest spell of all. I have but to point it at you or any of your monsters and they will fall dead as though blasted by a levin-bolt."

He held up the object with which he had been defending himself against the robbers, a two-foot bronze tube open at one end and closed at the other, and fastened by bronze straps to a piece of carved wood extending beyond the closed end and terminating in a squared-off butt.

The elder Seteshan roused himself from his stupor again. "That is interesting, Galathan," he said. "While I am all Qahura says and more, never have I seen a wand like that. How does it work?"

Ghw took a big gulp of wine, hiccupped, and fumbled in his scrip. He brought out a fistful of a dark granular substance and poured it down the open end of the tube.

"One inserts this magical powder thus," he said. "Then one drops this leaden ball, molded to fit loosely into the tube, down upon the powder—thus. One thrusts down a wad of rag to hold the ball in place—thus. One sprinkles a little of the powder in at this small hole—thus. Then one lights the powder with any convenient flame, and with a mighty flash and thunderclap the ball is driven through any object standing in the way. Fear not; I value the stuff too highly to waste it in mere demonstration before a pair of degenerate mountebanks."

"Why didn't you use it on the thieves?" asked Suar.

"Because it was not charged, and even if it had been, I had no fire wherewith to set it off."

The pin-points of Semkaf's eyes stared unwinkingly at the contraption. "And what," he purred, "is the composition of the powder?"

Ghw wagged his head with drunken solemnity. "That you shall never learn from me! It was confided to me by our lamented archdruid just before his mischance. When he lay dying from the cut he had unwittingly given himself, he bequeathed to me the device and all its secrets."

Midawan the smith, who hitherto had been too busy eating to take part in the conversation, spoke up. "I don't like your magical device, stranger. With power enough behind that ball it would pierce my strongest shield or breastplate. Then where would my trade be? At the bottom of the ocean!"

"High time, too," said Suar. "With these improvements in armor the fine old art of fence is dying out. Now that men fight laden like lobsters with bronze plates and scales, they prefer to the rapier these clumsy broadswords to batter through the foe's defense. Mere woodcutter's strokes, chop-chop."

"Times change, and one must change with them," said Midawan.

"True, but that also applies to you," said Suar. "So you had better start working up a line of bronze lanterns and mirrors against the day when these things will have swept armor off the battlefield."

Semkaf leaned forward towards Ghw Gleokh. "I wish your device, mortal. Give it to me."

"Why, you insolent knave!" replied Ghw. "Are you mad? We slay men for less."

"Gentlemen!" said Suar. "Not here, pray! Or at least wait until I finish giving them the *Song of Vrir* and have collected my bounty. I'll rend your hearts with emotion. . . ." He hastily tuned his lyre.

Semkaf said, "What are your songs to me? I have no mortal emotions. I wish—"

"So you're like these greedy Kernean swine?" said Suar. "No appreciation of the arts; all they care for is trade-metal. Anyway, the device will do you no good without the formula for the powder."

"I can learn that through my arts at my leisure," said Semkaf. "Come, friend Ghw, I offer you in return that which is of the very highest value to you."

"And what is that, buffoon?" said Ghw.

"Only your life."

Ghw spat across the table, and followed this gesture by picking up his blackjack and throwing the lees of his wine into the Seteshan's face. "That for you!"

Semkaf wiped his narrow face with the edge of his cloak and turned his hawklike head towards his apprentice, murmuring, "These savages weary me. Slay them, Qahura."

Qahura wetted a finger in the spilt wine, drew a symbol on the table, and began to incant. Before the first sentence in the unknown tongue had rolled out, however, Ghw Gleokh raised the tube device in his right hand and set the wooden stock against his shoulder, so that the open end of the tube pointed towards Qahura's chest. With his left hand he picked up the rush-light and applied the flame to the little hole in the top of the tube.

There was a fizz, and a plume of yellow flame and sparks shot up from the hole. Almost instantly the room rocked to the crash of a tremendous explosion. Flame and smoke vomited out from the open end of the tube, hiding Qahura from view.

While the room still rang with the echoes of the report, every other face in the tavern turned towards Suar's table. Then there were hoarse yells and the clatter of overturning tables and benches as the rest of the customers fought to get out, trampling one another in their panic. The cat conjured up by Qahura had vanished at the instant of the explosion. Suar coughed at the smell of burnt sulfur.

As the smoke cleared, Qahura, his eyelids drooping

and his mouth hanging slackly open, fell forward across the table and lay with his smoke-blackened face in the spilt wine. Over his body, Semkaf and Ghw stared at one another. Ghw had dropped the tube and snatched up the broadsword that he had taken from the thief but now he seemed to be struggling in the grip of some strange paralysis. Suar tried to rise, but found that he had goten his legs entangled with the bench and with his cloak and his rapier.

"I underestimated you," said Semkaf, slipping a ring of reptilian form off his finger and making mystical motions with it. "*Antif maa-yb, 'oth-m-hru, Apepite!*"

Suar became aware of a horrid reptilian stench and the dry slither of scales. He saw nothing, but on his right hand, Midawan the smith recoiled as from an unseen contact and Ghw Gleokh screamed an unearthly shriek. Something caught hold of the Galathan and dragged him off his bench to the floor. Suar, still trying to gain his feet, was astonished to observe that the ex-druid's right arm had vanished up to the shoulder.

The other customers had now nearly all crowded out through every aperture in the building. In a moment they were gone.

Midawan in one hulking motion drew a big broad knife from his belt and vaulted over the table diagonally from where he sat at the end, coming down almost in Suar's lap in the place where Ghw had sat. As he alighted, his right arm lashed out and drove the knife into Semkaf's chest, cutting into the middle of another sentence of anathema and scorcerous doom.

On the floor, Ghw was undergoing strange convulsions, as if some immense and invisible snake were squeezing him to death. His body bent and thrashed; blood spurted and bones cracked like sticks.

Suar got untangled from his gear, stepped back over the bench, and started for the door. He and Midawan were the last persons in the room except for the three magicians. As Suar ran for the door, trailing his cloak and hugging his precious lyre, he paused to look back.

Semkaf now lay forward, facedown across the table like his apprentice beside him. On the floor Ghw Gleokh, bloody and distorted, had ceased to flop and writhe. He lay quietly, but now his head and most of his other arm had also vanished. In that last glance Suar saw the zone of invisibility slip down until only the lower half of Ghw's body and his legs were visible. Just as if one were watching a frog being swallowed head-first by an invisible snake. . . .

Outside, Suar and Midawan raced three blocks through the wet along Ocean Street before stopping to breathe. Suar asked, "Why did you kill Semkaf? It wasn't really our quarrel."

"Didn't you hear him tell Qahura to slay the lot of us? These he-witches are not nice in dealing out their dooms."

"How were you able to do it when Ghw was not?"

"I really don't know. I suppose because I was careful not to look him in the eye, and perhaps he was weak from the effects of that drug he was inhaling; the rose-of-death, if I know the smell."

"But now his private fiend is loose without a master to banish it back to its own world!"

Midawan shrugged. "Those things usually go back of their own accord, I'm told. If we hear that Apepis is still slithering around town tomorrow we can go off to visit my cousins in Tegrazen. Besides, Semkaf would have learned the secrets of the thunder-tube, and if the thing had come into general use, that would have been bad for my trade."

Suar Peial became aware that Midawan was carrying

the tube-device in question. As he spoke, the smith threw the thing gyrating far out into the bay. Suar heard a faint splash as it struck the water invisibly in the dark and sank.

"*Hé*," said Suar. "If you didn't want it, I could have sold the bronze for the price of several meals. As I had no chance to sing tonight, Lyr only knows when I shall eat again, let alone drink a skin of wine or bounce a wench."

"Such things are better out of reach," said Midawan. "And I can stake you to a meal or two. Not that it really worries me, you understand. We should have to improve our craft, no doubt; but no magical toy like that will ever put us out of business. Yes, sir, armor is here to stay!"

*Today we only "know" Atlantis in legend
or in fable, and through the writings of
those few who have tried to piece together
the scattered remains of past civilizations
and empires by now forgotten by time. At
one stage in the history of Atlantis, before
it was to become nothing but a legend
known only to the very old, men such as
Elak must have lived and laughed and
fought—and died. . . .*

# DRAGON MOON

## by Henry Kuttner

# DRAGON MOON

### 1. *Elak of Atlantis*

Of great limbs gone to chaos,
  A great face turned to night—
Why bend above a shapeless shroud
Seeking in such archaic cloud
  Sight of strong lords and light?

—Chesterton

THE wharf-side tavern was a bedlam. The great harbor of Poseidonia stretched darkly to the southeast, but the waterfront was a blaze of bright lanterns and torches. Ships had made port today, and this tavern, like the others, roared with mirth and rough nautical oaths. Cooking-smoke and odor of sesame filled the broad low room, mingled with the sharp tang of wine. The swarthy seamen of the south held high carnival tonight.

In a niche in the wall was an image of the patron god, Poseidon of the sunlit seas. It was noticeable that before swilling liquor, nearly every man spilled a drop or two on the floor in the direction of the carved god.

A fat little man sat in a corner and muttered under his

breath. Lycon's small eyes examined the tavern with some distaste. His purse was, for a change, heavy with gold; so was that of Elak, his fellow adventurer. Yet Elak preferred to drink and wench in this brawling, smelly tavern, a predilection that filled Lycon with annoyance and bitterness. He spat, muttered under his breath, and turned to watch Elak.

The lean, wolf-faced adventurer was quarreling with a sea captain whose huge, great-muscled body dwarfed Elak's. Between the two a tavern wench was seated, her slanted eyes watching the men slyly, flattered by the attention given her.

The seaman, Drezzar, had made the mistake of underestimating Elak's potentialities. He had cast covetous eyes upon the wench and determined to have her, regardless of Elak's prior claim. Under other circumstances Elak might have left the slant-eyed girl to Drezzar, but the captain's words had been insulting. So Elak remained at the table, his gaze wary, and his rapier loosened in its scabbard.

He watched Drezzar, noting the sunburnt, massive face, the bushy dark beard, the crinkled scar that swept down from temple to jawbone, blinding the man in one gray eye. And Lycon called for more wine. Steel would flash soon, he knew.

Yet the battle came without warning. A stool was overturned, there was a flare of harsh oaths, and Drezzar's sword came out, flaming in the lamplight. The wench screamed shrilly and fled, having little taste for bloodshed save from a distance.

Drezzar feinted; his sword swept out in a treacherously low cut that would have disemboweled Elak had it reached its mark. But the smaller man's body writhed aside in swift, flowing motion; the rapier shimmered. Its point gashed Drezzar's scalp.

They fought in silence. And this, more than anything

else, gave Elak the measure of his opponent. Drezzar's face was quite emotionless. Only the scar stood out white and distinct. His blinded eye seemed not to handicap him in the slightest degree.

Lycon waited for a chance to sheathe his steel in Drezzar's back. Elak would disapprove, he knew, but Lycon was a realist.

Elak's sandal slipped in a puddle of spilled liquor, and he threw himself aside desperately, striving to regain his balance. He failed. Drezzar's lashing sword drove the rapier from his hand, and Elak went down, his head cracking sharply on an overturned stool.

The seaman poised himself, sighted down his blade, and lunged. Lycon was darting forward, but he knew he could not reach the killer in time.

And then—from the open door came the inexplicable. Something like a streak of flaming light lashed through the air, and at first Lycon thought it was a thrown dagger. But it was not. It was—flame!

White flame, darting and unearthly! It gripped Drezzar's blade, coiled about it, ripped it from the seaman's hand. It blazed up in blinding fiery light, limning the room in starkly distinct detail. The sword fell uselessly to the floor, a blackened, twisted stump of melted metal.

Drezzar shouted an oath. He stared at the ruined weapon, and his bronzed face paled. Swiftly he whirled and fled through a side door.

The flame had vanished. In the door a man stood—a gross, ugly figure clad in the traditional brown robe of the druids.

Lycon, skidding to a halt, lowered his sword and whispered, "Dalan!"

Elak got to his feet, rubbing his head ruefully. At sight of the druid his face changed. Without a word he nodded to Lycon and moved toward the door.

The three went out into the night.

## 2. *Dragon Throne*

Now we are come to our Kingdom,
And the Crown is ours to take—
With a naked sword at the Council board,
And under the throne the snake,
*Now we are come to our Kingdom!*

—Kipling

"I bring you a throne," Dalan said, "but you must hold it with your blade."

They stood at the end of a jetty, looking out at the moonlit harbor waters. The clamor of Poseidonia seemed far away now.

Elak stared at the hills. Beyond them, leagues upon leagues to the north, lay a life he had put behind him. A life he had given up when he left Cyrena to gird on an adventurer's blade. In Elak's veins ran the blood of the kings of Cyrena, northernmost kingdom of Atlantis. And, but for a fatal quarrel with his stepfather, Norian, Elak would have been on the dragon throne even then. But Norian had died, and Elak's brother, Orander, took the crown.

Elak said, "Orander rules Cyrena. Do you ask me to join a rebellion against my brother?" An angry light showed in the adventurer's cold eyes.

"Orander is dead," the druid said quietly. "Elak, I have a tale to tell you, a tale of sorcery and black evil that has cast its shadow over Cyrena. But first—" He fumbled in his shapeless brown robe and drew forth a tiny crystal sphere. He cupped it in his palm, breathed upon it. The clear surface clouded, misted—and the fog seemed to permeate the entire globe. The druid held a ball of whirling gray cloud in his hand.

Within the sphere a picture grew, microscopic but vividly distinct. Elak peered closely. He saw a throne, and a man who sat upon it.

"South of Cyrena, beyond the mountains, lies Kiriath," Dalan said. "Sepher ruled it. And now Sepher still sits upon his throne, but he is no longer human."

In the globe the face of Sepher sprang out in startling clarity. Involuntarily Elak drew back, his lips thinning. At a casual glance Sepher seemed unchanged, a black-bearded, bronzed giant with the keen eyes of a hawk, but Elak knew that he looked upon a creature loathsome beyond anything on earth. It was not evil, as he knew it, but a thing beyond good and evil as it was beyond humanity or deity. A Presence from Outside had touched Sepher and taken Kiriath's king for its own. And Elak knew this was the most horrible being he had ever seen.

Dalan hid the crystal. He said coldly, "Out of the unknown has come a being named Karkora. What he is I know not. I have cast the runes, and they say little to me. The altar fires have whispered of a shadow that will come upon Cyrena, a shadow that may spread over all Atlantis. Karkora, the Pallid One, is not human, nor is he a demon. He is—alien, Elak."

"What of my brother?" the adventurer asked.

"You have seen Sepher," Dalan said. "He is possessed, a vessel of this entity called Karkora. Ere I left Orander, he, too, had—changed."

A muscle twitched in Elak's brown cheek. The druid went on.

"Orander saw his doom. Day by day the power of Karkora over him increased, and the soul of your brother was driven further into the outer dark. He died—by his own hand."

Elak's face did not change expression. But for minutes he was silent, a deep sorrow in his gray eyes.

Lycon turned to look out across the sea.

The druid went on, "Orander sent a message to you, Elak. You, in all Atlantis, are of the royal line of Cyrena. Yours, therefore, is the crown. It will not be easy to hold. Karkora is not defeated. But my magic will aid you."

Elak said, "You offer me the dragon throne?"

Dalan nodded.

"The years have changed me, Dalan. I have gone through Atlantis a vagabond and worse. I put my birthright behind me and forgot it. And I'm not the same man who went from Cyrena years ago," Elak said softly, laughing a little bitterly, and looking over the jetty's edge at his face reflected in the dark swell of the water. "Only a king may sit on the dragon throne. For me—it would be a jest. And a sorry one."

"You fool!" the druid whispered—and there was rage in his words. "Blind, mad fool! Do you think the druids would offer Cyrena to the wrong man? Blood of kings is in your veins, Elak. It is not yours to deny. You must obey."

"Must?" The word was spoken lightly, yet Lycon felt a tenseness go through him, tightening his muscles. "Must?" Elak asked.

"The decision is mine, druid. By Mider! The throne of Cyrena means much to me. Therefore I shall not sit in it!"

Dalan's toad face was gargoylish in the moonlight. He thrust his bald, glistening head forward, and his thick, stubby fingers twisted.

"Now am I tempted to work magic on you, Elak," he said harshly. "I am no—"

"I have given you my answer."

The druid hesitated. His somber eyes dwelt on Elak. Then, without a word, he turned and went lumbering off into the night. His footsteps died.

Elak remained staring out at the harbor. His cheeks were gray, his mouth a tortured white line. And he whirled, abruptly, and looked at the hills of Poseidonia.

But he did not see them. His gaze went beyond them, far and far, probing through all Atlantis to the kingdom of the north—Cyrena, and the dragon throne.

### 3. *The Gates of Dream*

Churel and ghoul and Djinn and sprite
Shall bear us company tonight,
For we have reached the Oldest Land
Wherein the powers of Darkness range.

—Kipling

Elak's sleep that night was broken by dreams—flashing, disordered visions of many things. He stared up at the white moonlit ceiling of the apartment. And—it was changed. The familiar room was gone. Light still existed, but it was oddly changed—grayish and unreal. Unearthly planes and angles slipped past Elak, and in his ears a low humming grew. This changed to a high-pitched, droning whine, and died away at last.

The mad planes reassembled themselves. In his dream Elak saw a mighty crag upthrust against cold stars—colossal against a background of jagged mountain peaks. Snow dappled them, but the darkness of the crag was unbroken. On its top was a tower, dwarfed by distance.

A flood seemed to lift Elak and bear him swiftly forward. In the base of the crag, he saw, were great iron gates. And these parted and swung aside, yawning for him as he moved through.

They shut silently behind him.

And now Elak became conscious of a Presence. It was stygian black; yet in the tenebrous darkness there was a

73

vague inchoate stirring, a sense of motion that was unmistakable.

Without warning Elak saw—the Pallid One!

A white and shining figure flashed into view. How tall it was, how close or distant, the man could not tell. Nor could he see more than the bare outline. A crawling, leprous shimmer of cold light rippled over the being; it seemed little more than a white shadow. But a shadow—three-dimensional, alive!

The unearthly terror of Karkora, the Pallid One!

The being seemed to grow larger. Elak knew he was watched, coldly and dispassionately. His senses were no longer dependable. It did not seem as though he beheld Karkora with his eyes alone—he was no longer conscious of his body.

He remembered Dalan, and Dalan's god. And he cried silently upon Mider for aid.

The shuddering loathing that filled him did not pass, but the horror that tore at his mind was no longer as strong. Again he cried to Mider, forcing himself to concentrate on the Druid god.

Once more Elak called out to Mider. And, silently, eerily, a wall of flame rose about him, shutting off the vision of Karkora. The warm, flickering fires of Mider were a protective barrier—earthly, friendly.

They closed in—drew him back. They warmed the chill horror that froze his mind. They changed to sunlight—and the sunlight was slanting in through the window, beside which Elak lay on his low bed, awake and shuddering with reaction.

"By the Nine Hells!" he cursed, leaping up swiftly. "By all the gods of Atlantis! Where's my rapier?" He found it, and whirled it hissing through the air. "How can a man battle dreams?"

He turned to Lycon, slumbering noisily nearby, and kicked the small man into wakefulness.

74

"Hog-swill," said Lycon, rubbing his eyes. "Bring another cup, and swiftly, or I'll—eh? What's wrong?"

Elak was dressing hastily. "What's wrong? Something I didn't expect. How could I know from Dalan's words the sort of thing that's come to life in Atlantis?" He spat in disgust. "That leprous foulness shall never take the dragon throne!"

He slammed his rapier into its scabbard. "I'll find Dalan. I'll go back with him. To Cyrena."

Elak was silent, but deep in his eyes was a black horror and loathing. He had seen the Pallid One. And he knew that never in words could he hope to express the burning foulness of alien Karkora.

But Dalan had vanished. It was impossible to find the druid in teeming Poseidonia. And at last Elak gave up hope and determined to take matters into his own hands. A galley called *Kraken* was leaving that day, he learned, and would beat up the western coast. In fact, by the time Elak had hired a boatman to take him and Lycon to the vessel, the galley's oars were already dipping into the swells.

Elak's cockleshell gained its side, and he clambered over the gunwale, hoisting Lycon after him. He tossed a coin to the boatman and saw the man depart.

The sweating backs of slaves were moving rhythmically under the lash of the overseers. One of these came forward at a run, his bronzed face angry.

"Who are you?" he hailed. "What do you seek on the *Kraken?*"

"Take us to your captain," Elak said shortly. His hand touched the heavy purse at his belt, and coins jingled. The overseer was impressed.

"We're putting to sea," he said. "What do you want?"

"Passage to Cyrena," Lycon snapped. "Be—"

"Bring them here, Rasul," a gruff voice broke in. "They are friends. We'll give them passage to Cyrena— aye!"

75

And Drezzar, Elak's opponent in the tavern brawl, hastened along the poop toward them, teeth gleaming in his bushy beard.

"Ho!" he yelled at a nearby group of armed seamen. "Seize those two! Take them—alive! You dog," Drezzar said with cold rage. He stood before Elak and lifted his hand as though to strike the captive.

Elak said stoically, "I want passage to Cyrena. I'll pay well for it."

"So you will," Drezzar grinned, and ripped off Elak's purse. He opened it and ran golden coins through his thick fingers. "You'll work for it, too. But you'll not reach Cyrena.

"Two more oarsmen for you, Rasul. Two more slaves.

"See that they work!"

He turned and strode away. Unresisting, Elak was dragged to a vacant oar and chained there, Lycon shackled beside him. His hands fell in well-worn grooves on the polished wood.

Rasul's whip cracked. The overseer called, "Pull! Pull!"

The *Kraken* sped seaward. And, chained to his oar, straining at the unaccustomed toil, Elak's dark wolf-face bore a smile that was not pleasant to see.


### 4. *The Ship Sails North*

Orpheus has harped her,
Her prow has sheared the spray,
Fifty haughty heroes at her golden oarlocks sway,
White the wave before her flings,
Bright from shore she lifts and swings,
Wild he twangs the ringing strings—
Give way! Give way!

—Benet

They drove down along the coast and skirted the southern tip of Atlantis. Then the galley crept northwest, up the long curve of the continent, and all the while the days were cloudless and fair, and the skies blue as the waters of the Ocean Sea.

Elak bided his time until the *Kraken* dropped anchor one afternoon at an uninhabited island, to replenish the water supply. Drezzar went ashore with a dozen others, leaving only a few men in charge of the ship. This was apparently safe enough, with the slaves chained. Moreover, Drezzar had the only keys. But, at sunset, Elak nudged Lycon awake and told him to keep watch.

"What for?" Lycon's voice was surly. "Do you—" He broke off, staring, as Elak took a tiny twisted bit of metal from his sandal and inserted it delicately in the lock of his ankle-cuff. "Gods!" Lycon cursed. "You had that all the time—and you waited till now!"

"These locks are easy to pick," Elak said. "What? Of course I waited! We've only a few enemies aboard now, instead of more than a dozen. Keep watch, I tell you."

Lycon obeyed. Footsteps creaked upon the deck occasionally, and there were lanterns here and there on the ship, but their illumination was faint enough. The lapping of water against the hull drowned the soft scrape and click as Elak worked. Presently he sighed in satisfaction and opened the cuff.

Metal clicked and scraped. Elak was free. He turned to Lycon—and then hurrying footsteps sounded on the raised deck. Rasul, the overseer, ran up, dragging his long whip. He peered down—and dragged out his sword, cursing. With the other hand he swept the whip in a great singing blow, smashing down on Elak's unprotected shoulders.

Lycon acted. In one swift motion he flung himself forward, guarding Elak; the lash ripped skin and flesh from Lycon's side. And then Elak's sinewy hand closed on the

77

tough hide; he pulled mightily—pulled it from Rasul's grasp.

"Ho!" the overseer shouted. "Ho! To me!" His voice roared out over the dark sea. His long sword was a pale flickering light in the glow of the lanterns.

Two more men, armed, came running up behind Rasul. They spread out and closed in on Elak. He grinned unpleasantly, as a wolf smiles. The whip was coiled in his hand.

It sprang out suddenly, like a striking snake. The fanged, vicious tip hissed shrilly. In the dimness the lash was difficult to see, impossible to dodge. Rasul roared in pain.

"Slay him!" the overseer shouted.

The three ran in, and Elak gave way, his wrist turning as he swung the whip. A thrown dagger brought blood from the Atlantean's shoulder. And a man staggered back, screaming shrilly, clawing at his eyes that were blinded by the tearing rip of the lash.

"Slay me, then," Elak whispered, cold laughter in his eyes. "But the dog's fangs are sharp, Rasul."

He caught a glimpse of Lycon, bent above his bonds, busily manipulating the bit of metal that would unlock them. Voices called from the shore. Rasul shouted a response, and then ducked and gasped as the whip shrieked through the dark air.

" 'Ware my fangs, Rasul!" Elak smiled mirthlessly.

And now the two—Rasul and his companion—were in turn giving way. Step by step Elak forced them back, under the threat of the terrible lash. They could not guard against it, could not see it. Out of the gloom it would come striking, swift as a snake's thrust, leaping viciously at their eyes. The slaves were awake and straining in their chains, calling encouragement to Elak. The man who had been blinded made a misstep and fell among the rowers. They surged up over him; lean hands reached and clawed in the lantern-light. He screamed for a time, and then made no further sound.

Lycon's voice rose, shrill and peremptory, above the tumult.

"Row!" he yelped. "Row, slaves! Ere Drezzar returns —row for your freedom!" Alternately he cursed and threatened and cajoled them, and worked at his bonds with flying fingers.

Elak heard a whisper at his side, saw a slave thrusting a sword at him, hilt-first—the blade the blinded one had dropped. Gratefully he seized it, hurling the whip away. The feel of the cool, leather-bound hilt was grateful. Tide of strength surged up Elak's arm from the sharp steel.

It was not his rapier—but it would do.

"My fangs, Rasul," he said, laughing—and ran in. His two opponents spread out, but he had foreseen that move. He turned his back on Rasul, cut at the other, and almost in the same motion whirled and leaped past, dodging a thrust by a hair's-breadth. And now Rasul only faced him. The other man was down, tearing at a throat sliced through to the spine.

Lycon shouted, "Row, slaves! For your lives!"

The long oars clacked and moved in confusion; then habit stepped in, and rhythmically, slowly, the blades dug into the sea. Lycon yelled a chant, and the slaves kept time to it. Gradually the galley gained way.

On the deck swords flamed and clashed. But Elak was not fated to slay Rasul. The overseer stumbled, dropped to one knee—and hands reached for him out of the dark. Shouting, he was dragged down among the slaves. Voices rose to a yelping crescendo of hate. Rasul screamed— and was silent.

Lycon leaped up, free from his chains. He cursed the rowers; their momentary inattention to their duty had caused confusion. An oar, caught among others, splintered and broke. The butt bent like a bow, snapped back, and smashed a slave's face to bloody ruin. From overside came cries and commands.

The face of Drezzar rose above the rail, hideous, contorted, the scar flaming red. He gripped his sword between his teeth. After him armed men came pouring.

Lycon, a captured blade bare in his hand, ran toward them, yelling objurgations at the slaves. The oars moved again, tore at the sea, sent the galley through the waves once more. A slave had long since cut the anchor-rope.

A dozen armed men, swords gleaming, were ringed about Lycon, who, his back against the mast, was valiantly battling and cursing in lurid oaths. A few steps away Drezzar came catlike, and murder was in his eyes. He saw Elak stir, and ran in, blade ready.

Elak did not stoop to recover his sword. He sprang forward, under the sweep of the steel, which Drezzar had not expected. The two men went down together, rolling on the blood-slippery deck.

Drezzar tried to reverse the sword in his hand and stab Elak in the back. But Elak's supple body writhed aside, and simultaneously his lean, sinewy fingers closed on Drezzar's, above the hilt of the blade.

Drezzar tried to turn the blow, but could not. Elak continued his enemy's thrust. And the sword went smoothly into Drezzar's belly, without pausing till it grated against the backbone.

"My fangs, Drezzar," Elak said very softly, and with no expression on his wolf-face—and then drove the sword further in till it pinned the captain, like a beetle, to the deck. Drezzar's mouth opened; a roaring exhalation of breath, fraught with ghastly agony, seemed torn out of the man. His hands beat the deck; his body doubled up and arched like a bow.

He coughed blood, gnashed his teeth till they splintered and cracked—and so died.

80

Elak sprang up. He saw a heavy iron key hanging at Drezzar's belt. This he tore away and cast down among the slaves. A grateful clamor came in response.

Lycon called frantically for aid. Elak responded. But now the outcome of the battle was a foregone conclusion. One by one the freed slaves passed the iron key to their neighbors and came springing up to add their numbers to Elak's cause. And, presently, the last of the ship's masters lay dead on deck, and the oarsmen—no longer in chains, no longer slaves—sent the galley plunging through the dark sea to the north.

## 5. Aynger of Amenalk

> For the man dwelt in a lost land
>    Of boulders and broken men . . .
>
> —Chesterton

They came to a forbidding, bleak coast that loomed high above the galley. The cold winds of autumn filled the sails and let the weary oarsmen rest. The sea turned smoothly gray, surging in long, foamless swells under a blue-gray sky. The sun gave little heat. The crew turned gratefully to the ship's stock—oil and wine and woven stuff, finding warmth and comfort in it.

But Elak was chafed by inaction. He longed to reach Cyrena; endlessly he paced the decks, fingering his rapier and pondering on the mystery of the thing called Karkora. What was this Pallid One? Whence had it come? These problems were insoluble, and remained so till, one night, Elak dreamed.

He dreamed of Dalan. The druid priest seemed to be standing in a forest glade; before him a fire flickered redly. And Dalan said:

"Leave your ship at the red delta. Seek Aynger of Amenalk. Tell him you seek the throne of Cyrena!"

There was no more. Elak awoke, listening to the creaking of the galley's timbers and the whisper of waves against the side. It was nearly dawn. He rose, went on deck, and searched the horizon under a shielding palm.

To the right, breaking the gray cliffs, was a gap. Beyond it—an island. And on the island a castle loomed, part of the rock, it seemed, growing from it.

The galley swept on. And now Elak saw that a river ran between the broken cliffs. At its mouth was a delta, made of reddish sand.

So, in the cold, lowering dawn, Elak and Lycon left the galley. Willing oarsmen rowed them to shore. The two climbed the northern cliff and stood staring around. Inland the plateau stretched unbroken by tree or bush, windswept and desolate. To the west lay the Ocean Sea, chill and forbidding.

"Perhaps this Aynger of your dream dwells in that castle," Lycon said, pointing and shivering. "One of the men told me this is Kiriath. To the north, beyond the mountains, lies Cyrena."

Elak said somberly, "I know. And Sepher rules over Kiriath—Sepher, whom Karkora has taken for his own. Well—come on."

They set out along the edge of the cliff. The wind blew coldly, and brought to them a thin, high piping that seemed to come out of nowhere. Sad, mournful, weird, it murmured half-heard in the air about the two.

And across the plateau a man came—a great gray man, roughly clad, with unkempt hair and iron-gray beard. He played upon a set of pipes, but put these away as he saw Elak and Lycon. He came closer and halted, with folded arms, waiting.

The man's face might have been chipped from the

82

rough rocks of this land. It was harsh and strong and forbidding, and the cool gray eyes were like the sea.

"What do you seek here?" he asked. His voice was deep and not at all unpleasant.

Elak hesitated. "Aynger. Aynger of Amenalk. Do you know of him?"

"I am Aynger."

For a heartbeat there was silence. Then Elak said, "I seek the throne of Cyrena."

Laughter sprang into the gray eyes. Aynger of Amenalk reached out a huge hand and gripped Elak's arm, squeezing it painfully. He said, "Dalan sent you! Dalan!"

Elak nodded.

"But it is not me you seek. It is Mayana—the daughter of Poseidon. You must seek her there." He pointed to the distant castle on the island. "Her power alone can aid you. But first—come."

He led the way to the cliff's edge. A perilous, narrow path led down the jagged face; Aynger started along it with sure-footed ease, and Elak and Lycon followed more gingerly. Far below, the breakers tore upon the rocks; seabirds called shrilly.

The path ended at a cave-mouth. Aynger entered, beckoning to the others. The cavern widened into a high-arched chamber, obviously Aynger's home. He gestured to a heap of furs and gave each of his guests a great horn of mead.

"So. Dalan sent you. I had wondered. Orander is dead. Once the Pallid One has set his seal on a man, there is escape in death alone."

"Karkora," Elak said musingly. "What is he? Do you know, Aynger?"

"You must seek your answer from Mayana, on the isle. Only she knows. Mayana—of the seas. Let me tell you." The gray eyes grew bright with dream. A softness crept into the deep voice. "This land, on the western shore, is Amenalk. Not Kiriath. Once, long ago, Amenalk stretched far to the east. We were a great people then. But invaders come conquering, and now only this bit of land is left to us. Yet it is Amenalk. And I dwell here because in my veins runs the blood of kings."

Aynger flung back his gray, tousled head. "And for ages the castle on the isle had existed. None dwelt there. There were legends that even before the Amenalks held this land, an ancient sea-people made it their home. Sorcerers they were, warlocks and magicians. But they died and were forgotten. So, in time, my own people were scattered through Kiriath, and I dwelt here alone.

"Sepher ruled, well and wisely. One night he walked alone on the cliffs of Amenalk, and when he returned to his palace, he brought a bride with him. The bride was Mayana. Some say he found her in the island castle. Some say she rose from the waves. I think she is not human. She is one of the old sea-race—

"A shadow fell on the land. Out of the dark, out of the unknown, came Karkora. He took Sepher for his own. Mayana fled here, and dwells now in the castle, protected by her sorcery. And Karkora rules."

Aynger's gray beard jutted; his eyes were lambent pools. He said, "My people were a druid race. We worshipped great Mider, as I do now. And I tell you that Karkora is a foulness and a horror—an evil that will spread through all the world if the druids fail to destroy him. Mayana holds his secret. Mayana knows. You must go to her on her isle. For myself—" A mighty hand clenched. "I have king's blood, and my people live, though in bondage. I shall go through Kiriath and gather men. I think you will need armies, ere you sit on Cyrena's dragon throne. Well. I have an army for you, and for Mider."

Aynger reached behind him, brought out a huge war-hammer, bound with thongs. Laughter touched his grim face.

"We shall fight in the old way, woad-painted, without armor. And I think Helm-Breaker will taste blood again. If you get aid from Mayana—well. But with you or without you, man of Cyrena, Amenalk will go forth to battle!"

The great gray man towered against the cave-mouth, a grim, archaic figure, somehow strong with primeval menace. He stood aside, pointing.

"Your way lies there, to the isle. Mine lies inland. When we meet again, if we do, I shall have an army to give you."

Silently Elak moved past Aynger and went up the cliff path. Lycon trailed him. On the windy, treeless plateau he stood unmoving, while the gray giant passed him without a word and strode away, his war-hammer over one muscular shoulder, beard and hair flying in the wind.

Aynger grew small in the distance. Elak nodded to Lycon.

"I think we have a strong ally there. We'll need him. But now—this Mayana. If she can solve the riddle of Karkora, I'll find her though I have to swim."

"You won't have to," Lycon said, wiping his mouth. "Gods, that mead was good! There's a bridge to the isle —see? A narrow one, but it will serve. Unless she's set a dragon to guard it."

## 6. *Mayana*

By the tall obelisks, all seaweed-girt,
    Drift the pale dead of long and long ago,
Lovers and kings who may not more be hurt,
    Wounded by lips or by the dagger's blow.

*—The Sunken Towers*

From the cliff's edge a narrow bridge of rock jutted, a natural formation worn by wind and rain. It ended on a jagged ledge, at the back of which a black hole gaped. Elak said, "Lycon, wait here. I must take this road alone."

The little man disagreed profanely. But Elak was firm. "It will be safer. So we won't both fall into the same trap. If I'm not back by sundown, come after me—you may be of aid then." Lycon could not help but realize the truth of this. He shrugged fat shoulders.

"Very well. I'll wait in Aynger's cave. His mead was potent; I'm anxious to sample more. Luck, Elak."

Nodding, the Atlantean started along the bridge. He found it safer not to look down, but the surging roar of the breakers sounded disquietingly from beneath. Seabirds mewed and called. The wind tore at his swaying body.

But at last he was across, and felt the firm stability of the rocky ground under his sandals. Without a backward glance he entered the cave-mouth. Almost immediately outside sounds dimmed and quieted.

The road led down—a natural passage, seemingly, that turned and twisted in the rock. Sand was gritty underfoot, with bits of shell here and there. For a time it was dark, and then a greenish, vague luminous glow appeared, apparently emanated by the sand on which he trod.

It was utterly silent.

Still the tunnel led down, till Elak's feet felt moisture beneath him. He hesitated, staring around. The rocky walls were dewed and sweating. A dank, salty odor was strong in his nostrils. Loosening his rapier in its scabbard, he went on.

The green glow brightened. The passage turned; Elak rounded the corner, and stood motionless, staring. Before him a vast cavern opened.

It was huge and terrifyingly strange. From the low roof, stalactites hung in myriad shapes and colors over

86

the broad expanse of an underground lake. The green shining was everywhere. The weight of the island above seemed to press down suffocatingly, but the air, despite a salt sea-smell, was fresh enough.

At his feet a sandy half-moon of a beach reached down to the motionless surface of the water. Further out, he could see, far down, vague shadows that resembled sunken buildings—fallen peristyles and columns; and far away, in the center of the lake, was an island.

Ruined marble crowned it. Only in the center a small temple seemed unharmed; it rose from shattered ruins in cool, white perfection. All around it the dead and broken city lay, to the water's edge and beyond. A submerged, forgotten metropolis lay before Elak.

Silence, and the pale green expanse of the waveless lake.

Softly Elak called, "Mayana." There was no response.

Frowning, he considered the task before him. He felt an odd conviction that what he sought lay in the temple on the islet, but there was no way of reaching it save by swimming. And there was something ominous about the motionless green of the waters.

Shrugging, Elak waded out. Icy chill touched his legs, crept higher about his loins and waist. He struck out strongly. And at first there was no difficulty; he made good progress.

But the water was very cold. It was salt, and this buoyed him up somewhat; yet when he glanced at the islet it seemed no nearer. Grunting, Elak buried his face in the waters and kicked vigorously.

His eyes opened. He looked down. He saw, beneath him, the sunken city.

Strange it was, and weird beyond imagination, to be floating above the wavering outline of these marble ruins. Streets and buildings and fallen towers were below, scarcely veiled by the luminous waters, but possessing a

87

vague, shadowy indistinctness that made them half-unreal. A green haze clothed the city. A city of shadows—

And the shadows moved and drifted in the tideless sea. Slowly, endlessly, they crept like a stain over the marble. They took shape before Elak's eyes.

Not sea-shapes—no. The shadows of men walked in the sunken metropolis. With queer, drifting motion the shadows went to and fro. They met and touched and parted again in strange similitude of life.

Stinging, choking cold filled Elak's mouth and nostrils. He spluttered and struck out, realizing that he was far beneath the surface, that, unconsciously holding his breath, he had drifted into the depths. He fought his way up.

It was oddly difficult. Soft, clinging arms seemed to touch him; the water darkened. But his head broke the surface, and he drank deeply of the chill air. Only by swimming with all his strength could he keep from sinking. That inexplicable drag pulled him down.

He went under. His eyes were open, and he saw, far below, movement in the sunken city. The shadow-shapes were swirling up, rising, spinning like autumn leaves—rising to the surface. And shadows clustered about Elak, binding him with gossamer fetters. They clung feathery and tenacious as spider-webs.

The shadows drew him down into the shining depths.

He struck out frantically. His head broke water once more; he saw the islet, closer now.

"Mayana!" he called. "*Mayana!*"

Rustling movement shook the shadows. A ripple of mocking laughter seemed to go through them. They closed in again, dim, impalpable, unreal. Elak went under once more, too exhausted to fight, letting the shadows have their will with him. Only his mind cried out desperately to Mayana, striving to summon her to his aid.

The waters brightened. The green glow flamed emerald-bright. The shadows seemed to pause with odd hesitation, as though listening.

Then suddenly they closed in on Elak. They bore him through the waters; he was conscious of swift movement amid whirling green fire.

The shadows carried him to the islet, bore him up as on a wave, and left him upon the sands.

The green light faded to its former dimness. Choking, coughing, Elak clambered to his feet. He stared around.

The shadows had vanished. Only the motionless lake stretched in the distance. He stood amid the ruins of the islet.

Hastily he staggered away from the water's marge, clambering across broken plinths and fallen pillars, making his way to the central temple. It stood in a tiny plaza, unmarred by time, but stained and discolored in every stone.

The brazen door gaped open. Unsteadily Elak climbed the steps and paused at the threshold. He looked upon a bare room, lit with the familiar emerald glow, featureless save for a curtain, on the further wall, made of some metallic cloth and figured with the trident of the sea-god.

There was no sound but Elak's hastened breathing. Then, abruptly, a low splashing came from beyond the curtain. It parted.

Beyond it was green light, so brilliant it was impossible to look upon. Silhouetted against the brightness for a moment loomed a figure—a figure of unearthly slimness and height. Only for a second did Elak see it; then the curtain swung back into place and the visitant was gone.

Whispering through the temple came a voice, like the soft murmur of tiny, rippling waves. And it said:

"I am Mayana. Why do you seek me?"

# 7. Karkora

> And I saw a beast coming up
> out of the sea, having ten horns
> and seven heads, and on his
> horns ten diadems, and upon his
> heads names of blasphemy . . .
> and the dragon gave him his
> power, and his throne, and great
> authority.
>
> —Revelations 13:1

Elak's wet hand crept to his rapier. There had been no menace in the whisper, but it was strangely—inhuman. And the silhouette he had seen was not that of any earthly woman.

Yet he answered quietly enough, no tremor in his voice:

"I seek the dragon throne of Cyrena. And I come to you for aid against Karkora."

There was silence. When the whisper came again, it had in it all the sadness of waves and wind.

"Must I aid you? Against Karkora?"

"You know what manner of being he is?" Elak questioned.

"Aye—I know that well." The metallic curtain shook. "Seat yourself. You are tired—how are you named?"

"Elak."

"Elak, then—listen. I will tell you of the coming of Karkora, and of Erykion the sorcerer. And of Sepher, whom I loved." There was a pause; then the low whisper resumed.

"Who I am, what I am, you need not know, but you should understand that I am not entirely human. My ancestors dwelt in this sunken city. And I—well, for ten

90

years I took human shape and dwelt with Sepher as his wife. I loved him. And always I hoped to give him a son who would some day mount the throne. I hoped in vain, or so I thought.

"Now in the court dwelt Erykion, a wizard. His magic was not that of the sea, soft and kindly as the waves, but of a darker sort. Erykion delved in ruined temples and pored over forgotten manuscripts of strange lore. His vision went back even before the sea-folk sprang from the loins of Poseidon, and he opened the forbidden gates of Space and Time. He offered to give me a child, and I listened to him, to my sorrow.

"I shall not tell you of the months I spent in strange temples, before dreadful altars. I shall not tell you of Erykion's magic. I bore a son—dead."

The silver curtain shook; it was long before the unseen speaker resumed. "And this son was frightful. He was deformed in ways I cannot let myself remember. Sorcery had made him inhuman. Yet he was my son, my husband's son, and I loved him. When Erykion offered to give him life, I agreed to the price he demanded—even though the price was the child himself."

" 'I shall not harm him,' Erykion told me. 'Nay, I shall give him powers beyond those of any god or man. Some day he shall rule this world and others. Only give him to me, Mayana.' And I hearkened.

"Now of Erykion's sorcery I know little. Something had entered into the body of my son while I bore him, and what this thing was I do not know. It was dead, and it awoke. Erykion awoke it. He took this blind, dumb, maimed man-child and bore it to his home in the depths of the mountains. With his magic he deprived it of any vestige of the five senses. Only life remained, and the unknown dweller within.

"I remember something Erykion had once told me. 'We have in us a sixth sense, primeval and submerged, which can be very powerful once it is brought to light. I know how to do that. A blind man's hearing may become acute; his power goes to the senses remaining. If a child, at birth, be deprived of all five senses, his power will go to this sixth sense. My magic can insure that.' So Erykion made of my man-child a being blind and dumb and without consciousness, almost; for years he worked his spells and opened the gates of Time and Space, letting alien powers flood through. This sixth sense within the child grew stronger. And the dweller in his mind waxed great, unbound by the earthly fetters that bind humans. This is my son—my man-child—Karkora, the Pallid One!"

And silence. And again the whisper resumed.

"Yet it is not strange that I do not entirely hate and loathe Karkora. I know he is a burning horror and a thing that should not exist; yet I gave him birth. And so, when he entered the mind of Sepher, his father, I fled to this my castle. Here I dwell alone with my shadows. I strove to forget that once I knew the fields and skies and hearths of earth. Here, in my own place, I forgot.

"And you seek me to ask aid." There was anger in the soft murmur. "Aid to destroy that which came from my flesh!"

Elak said quietly, "Is Karkora's flesh—yours?"

"By Father Poseidon, no! I loved the human part of Karkora, and little of that is left now. The Pallid One is —is—he has a thousand frightful powers, through his one strange sense. It has opened for him gateways that should remain always locked. He walks in other worlds, beyond unlit seas, across the nighted voids beyond earth. And I know he seeks to spread his dominion over all. Kiriath fell to him, and I think Cyrena. In time he will take all Atlantis, and more than that."

Elak asked, "This Erykion, the wizard—what of him?"

"I do not know," Mayana said. "Perhaps he dwells in

his citadel yet, with Karkora. Not for years have I seen the sorcerer."

"Cannot Karkora be slain?"

There was a long pause. Then the whisper said, "I know not. His body, resting in the citadel, is mortal, but that which dwells within it is not. If you could reach the body of Karkora—even so you could not slay him."

"Nothing can kill the Pallid One?" Elak asked.

"Do not ask me this!" Mayana's voice said with angry urgency. "One thing, one talisman exists—and this I shall not and cannot give you."

"I am minded to force your talisman from you," Elak said slowly, "if I can. Yet I do not wish to do this thing."

From beyond the curtain came a sound that startled the man—a low, hopeless sobbing that had in it all the bleak sadness of the mournful sea. Mayana said brokenly:

"It is cold in my kingdom, Elak—cold and lonely. And I have no soul, only my life, while it lasts. My span is long, but when it ends there will be only darkness, for I am of the sea-folk. Elak, I have dwelt for a time on earth, and I would dwell there again, in green fields with the bright cornflowers and daisies gay amid the grass—with the fresh winds of earth caressing me. The hearth-fires, the sound of human voices, and a man's love—my Father Poseidon knows how I long for these again."

"The talisman," Elak said.

"Aye, the talisman. You may not have it."

Elak said very quietly, "What manner of world will this be if Karkora should rule?"

There was a shuddering, indrawn breath. Mayana said, "You are right. You shall have the talisman, if you should need it. I may be that you can defeat Karkora without it. I only pray that it may be so. Here is my word, then: in your hour of need, and not until then, I shall send you the talisman. And now go. Karkora has an earthly vessel in Sepher. Slay Sepher. Give me your blade, Elak."

Silently Elak unsheathed his rapier and extended it hilt-first. The curtain parted. Through it slipped a hand.

A hand—inhuman, strange! Very slender and pale it was, milk-white, with the barest suggestion of scales on the smooth, delicate texture of the skin. The fingers were slim and elongated, seemingly without joints, and filmy webs grew between them.

The hand took Elak's weapon and withdrew behind the curtain. Then it reappeared, again holding the rapier. Its blade glowed with a pale greenish radiance.

"Your steel will slay Sepher now. And it will give him peace." Elak gripped the hilt; the unearthly hand made a quick archaic gesture above the weapon.

"So I send a message to Sepher, my husband. And—Elak—kill him swiftly. A thrust through the eye into the brain will not hurt too much."

Then, suddenly, the hand thrust out and touched Elak upon the brow. He was conscious of a swift dizziness, a wild exaltation that surged through him in hot waves. Mayana whispered:

"You shall drink of my strength, Elak. Without it, you cannot hope to face Karkora. Stay with me for a moon—drinking the sea-power and Poseidon's magic."

"A moon—"

"Time will not exist. You will sleep, and while you sleep strength will pour into you. And when you awake, you may go forth to battle—strong!"

The giddiness mounted; Elak felt his senses leaving him. He whispered, "Lycon—I must give him a message—"

"Speak to him, then, and he will hear. My sorcery will open his ears."

Dimly, as though from far away, Elak heard Lycon's startled voice.

"Who calls me? Is it you, Elak? Where—I see no one on this lonely cliff."

"Speak to him!" Mayana commanded. And Elak obeyed.

"I am safe, Lycon. Here I must stay for one moon, alone. You must not wait. I have a task for you."

There was the sound of a stifled oath. "What task?"

"Go north to Cyrena. Find Dalan, or, failing that, gather an army. Cyrena must be ready when Kiriath marches. Tell Dalan, if you find him, what I have done, and that I will be with him in one moon. Then let the Druid guide your steps. And—Ishtar guide you, Lycon."

Softly came the far voice: "And Mother Ishtar be your shield. I'll obey. Farewell."

Green darkness drifted across Elak's vision.

Dimly, through closing eyes, he vaguely saw the curtain before him swept aside, and a dark silhouette moving forward—a shape slim and tall beyond human stature, yet delicately feminine withal. Mayana made a summoning gesture—and the shadows flowed into the temple.

They swept down upon Elak, bringing him darkness and cool, soothing quiet. He rested and slept, and the enchanted strength of the sea-woman poured into the citadel of his soul.

## 8. *The Dragon's Throne*

Dust of the stars was under our feet,
    glitter of stars above—
Wrecks of our wrath dropped reeling
        down as we fought and we
        spurned and we strove.
Worlds upon worlds we tossed aside,
    and scattered them to and fro,
The night that we stormed Valhalla, a
    million years ago!

—Kipling

The moon waxed and waned, and at last Elak awoke, on the further shore, by the cavern mouth that led to the upper world. The underground mere lay silent at his feet, still bathed in the soft green glow. In the distance the islet was, and he could make out the white outline of the temple upon it. The temple where he had slept for a month. But there was no sign of life. No shadows stirred in the depths beneath him. Yet within himself he sensed a secret well of power that had not been there before.

Pondering, he retraced his steps through the winding passage, across the rock bridge to the high ramp of the plateau. The plain was deserted. The sun was westering, and a cold wind blew bleakly from the sea.

Elak shrugged. His gaze turned north, and his hand touched the rapier-hilt.

"First, a horse," he grunted. "And then—Sepher! A blade for the king's throat!"

So within two hours a mercenary soldier lay dead, his blood staining a leathern tunic, and Elak galloped north on a stolen steed. Hard and fast he rode, through Kiriath, and whispers were borne to his ears on the gusting winds. Sepher was no longer in his city, they said. At the head of a vast army he was sweeping north to the Gateway, the mountain pass that led to Cyrena. From the very borders of Kiriath warriors were coming in answer to the king's summons; mercenaries and adventurers flooded in to serve under Sepher. He paid well and promised rich plunder—the sack of Cyrena.

A trail of blood marked Elak's path. Two horses he rode to death. But at last the Gateway lay behind him; he had thundered through Sharn Forest and forded Monra River. Against the horizon towered a battlemented castle, and this was Elak's goal. Here Orander had ruled. Here was the dragon throne, the heart of Cyrena.

Elak rode across the drawbridge and into the courtyard. He cast his mount's reins to a gaping servitor, leaped from the horse, and raced across the yard. He knew each step of the way. In this castle he had been born.

And now the throne room, vast, high-ceilinged, warm with afternoon sunlight. Men were gathered there. Princes and lords of Cyrena. Barons, dukes, minor chieftains. By the throne—Dalan. And beside him, Lycon, round face set in unaccustomed harsh lines, for once sober and steady on his feet.

"By Mider!" Lycon roared. "Elak! *Elak!*"

The Atlantean pushed his way through the murmuring, undecided crowd. He came to stand beside the throne. His hand gripped Lycon's shoulder and squeezed painfully. The little man grinned.

"Ishtar be praised," Lycon murmured. "Now I can get drunk again."

Dalan said, "I watched you in the crystal, Elak. But I could not aid. The magic of the Pallid One battled my own. Yet I think you have other magic now—sea-sorcery." He turned to the mob. His lifted arms quieted them.

"This is your king," Dalan said.

Voices were raised, some in approbation, some in angry protest and objection. A tall, lean oldster shouted, "Aye—this is Zeulas, returned once more. This is Orander's brother."

"Be silent, Hira," another snapped. "This scarecrow Cyrena's king?"

Elak flushed and took a half-step forward. Dalan's voice halted him.

"You disbelieve, Gorlias?" he asked. "Well—d'you know of a worthier man? Will you sit on the dragon throne?"

Gorlias looked at the Druid with an oddly frightened

air; he fell silent and turned away. The others broke into a renewed chorus of quarreling.

Hira silenced them. His lean face was triumphant. "There's one sure test. Let him take it."

He turned to Elak. "The lords of Cyrena have fought like a pack of snarling dogs since Orander's death. Each wanted the throne. Baron Kond yelled louder than the rest. Dalan offered him the dragon throne, in the name of Mider, if he could hold it."

From the others a low whisper went up—uneasy, fearful. Hira continued: "Kond mounted the dais a month ago and sat on the throne. And he died! The fires of Mider slew him."

"Aye," Gorlias whispered. "Let this Elak sit upon the throne!"

A chorus of assent rose. Lycon looked worried.

He murmured, "It's true, Elak. I saw it. Red fire came out of nowhere and burned Kond to a cinder."

Dalan was silent, his ugly face impassive. Elak, watching the druid, could not read a message in the shallow black eyes.

Gorlias said, "If you can sit on the throne, I'll follow you. If not—you'll be dead. Well?"

Elak did not speak. He turned and mounted the dais. For a moment he paused before the great throne of Cyrena, his gaze dwelling on the golden dragon that writhed across its back, the golden dragons on the arms. For ages the kings of Cyrena had ruled from this seat, ruled with honor and chivalry under the dragon. And now Elak remembered how, in Poseidonia, he had felt unworthy to mount the throne.

Would the fires of Mider slay him if he took his dead brother's place?

Silently Elak prayed to his god. "If I'm unworthy," he told Mider, with no thought of irreverence, but as one warrior to another, "then slay me, rather than let the throne be dishonored. Yours is the judgment."

He took his place on the dragon throne.

Silence fell like a pall on the great room. The faces of the crowd were intent and strained. Lycon's breath came fast. The druid's hands, hidden under the brown robe, made a quick, furtive gesture; his lips moved without sound.

Red light flashed out above the throne. Through the room a cry rose and mounted, wordless, fearful. The fires of Mider flamed up in glaring brilliance and cloaked Elak!

They hid him in a twisting crimson pall. They swirled about him, blazing with hot radiance.

They swept into a strange, fantastic shape—a coiling silhouette that grew steadily more distinct.

A dragon of flame coiled itself about Elak!

And suddenly it was gone. Lycon was gasping oaths. The others were milling about in a confused mob. Dalan stood motionless, smiling slightly.

And on the dragon throne Elak sat unharmed! No breath of fire had scorched or blistered him; no heat had reddened his skin. His eyes were blazing; he sprang up and unsheathed his rapier. Silently he lifted it.

There was a clash of ringing blades. A forest of bright steel lifted. A great shout bellowed out.

The lords of Cyrena swore allegiance to their king!

Now, however, Elak found that his task had scarcely begun. The armies of Sepher were not yet in Cyrena; the king of Kiriath was waiting beyond the mountain barrier till he had gathered his full strength. But he would march soon, and Cyrena must by then be organized to resist him.

"Karkora didn't invade Kiriath," Elak said to Dalan one day as they rode through Sharn Forest. "He invaded the mind of the king instead. Why does he depend on armies to conquer Cyrena?"

Dalan's shapeless brown robe flapped against his horse's flanks. "Have you forgotten Orander? He tried there,

99

and failed. Then there was no single ruler here. If he'd stolen the mind of Kond or Gorlias he'd still have had the other nobles against him. And conquer Cyrena he must, for it's the stronghold of Mider and the Druids. Karkora knows he must destroy us before he can rule this world and others, as he intends. So he uses Sepher and Kiriath's army. Already he's given orders to slaughter each druid."

"What of Aynger?" Elak demanded.

"A message came from him today. He has gathered his Amenalks in the mountains beyond the Gateway. They wait for our word. Barbarians, Elak—but good allies. They fight like mad wolves."

Cyrena rose to arms. From steading and farm, castle and citadel, city and fortress, the iron men came streaming. The roads glittered with bright steel and rang to the clash of horses' hoofs. The dragon banners fluttered in the chill winds of winter.

Rise and arm! In the name of Mider and the Dragon, draw your blade! So the messengers called; so the word went forth. Rise against Kiriath and Sepher!

The defending swords of Cyrena flashed bright. They thirsted for blood.

And Sepher of Kiriath rode north against the Dragon.

## 9. *The Hammer of Aynger*

And a strange music went with him,
Loud and yet strangely far;
The wild pipes of the western land,
Too keen for the ear to understand,
Sang high and deathly on each hand
When the dead man went to war.

—Chesterton

The first snows of winter lay white on the Gateway. All around towered the tall, frosted peaks of the mountain barrier, and a bitter wind gusted strongly through the pass. Within a month deep snow and avalanches would make the Gateway almost impassable.

The sky was cloudless, of chill pale blue. In the thin air everything stood out in startling clarity; voices carried far, as did the crunching of snow underfoot and the crackle of rocks deep-bitten by the iron cold.

The pass was seven miles long, and narrow in only a few spots. For the most part it was a broad valley bounded by the craggy cliffs. Canyons opened into it.

Dawn had flamed and spread in the east. The sun hung above a snow-capped peak. South of a narrow portion of the Gateway, part of Cyrena's army waited. Behind them were reinforcements. Upon the crags were archers and arbalesters, waiting to rain death upon the invaders. Steel-silver moved against a background of white snow and black grim rocks.

Elak was astride a war-horse upon a small hillock. Hira rode up, gaunt old face keenly alert, joy of battle in the faded eyes. He saluted swiftly.

"The bowmen are placed and ready," he said. "We've got rocks and boulders into position to crush Sepher's army, should it get too far."

Elak nodded. He wore chain-armor, gold encrusted, with a close-fitting helm of gleaming steel. His wolf face was taut with excitement, and he curbed the steed as it curvetted.

"Good, Hira. You are in command there. I trust your judgment."

As Hira departed, Dalan and Lycon arrived, the latter flushed and unsteady in his saddle. He gripped a drinking-horn and swilled mead from it occasionally. His long sword slapped the horse's flank.

"The minstrels will make a song of this battle," he observed. "Even the gods will eye it with some interest."

"Don't blaspheme," Dalan said, and turned to Elak. "I've a message from Aynger. His savage Amenalks wait in that side canyon—" The druid flung out a pointing hand—"and will come when we need them."

"Aye," Lycon broke in, "I saw them. Madmen and demons! They've painted themselves blue as the sky and are armed with scythes and flails and hammers, among others things. And they're playing tunes on their pipes and bragging, each louder than the other. Only Aynger sits silent, fondling his Helm-Breaker. He looks like an image chipped out of gray stone."

At the memory Lycon shivered and then gulped the rest of the mead. "Faith," he said sadly, "the horn's empty. Well, I must get more." And off he went, reeling in the saddle.

"Drunken little dog," Elak remarked. "But his hand will be steady enough on the sword."

Far away, a trumpet shouted shrilly, resounding among the peaks. Now the foreguard of Sepher's army was visible as a glitter of steel on casques and lifted spearheads. Along the pass they came, steadily, inexorbly, in close battle formation. The trumpet sang and skirled.

In response, drums of Cyrena snarled answer. They rose to a throbbing, menacing roar. Cymbals clashed resoundingly. The banners of the dragon flung out stiffly in the cold blast.

Kiriath rode without a standard. In silence, save for the clashing of metallic hoofs and the angry screaming of the trumpet, they came, a vast array that flooded into the valley. Pikemen, archers, knights, mercenaries—on they came, intent on conquest and plunder. Elak could not see Sepher, though his gaze searched for the king.

And slowly the invaders increased their speed, almost

102

imperceptibly at first, and then more swiftly till through the Gateway Kiriath charged and thundered, lances lowered, swords flashing. The trumpet shouted urgent menace.

Dalan's gross body moved uneasily in his saddle. He unsheathed his long blade.

Elak looked around. Behind him the army waited. Everything was ready.

The king of Cyrena rose in his stirrups. He lifted his rapier and gestured with it. He shouted:

*"Charge! Ho—the Dragon!"*

With a roar, Cyrena swept forward down the pass. Closer and closer the two vast forces came. The drums roared death. From the icy peaks the clamor resounded thunderously.

A cloud of arrows flew. Men fell, screaming. Then, with a crash that seemed to shake the mountainous walls of the Gateway, the armies met.

It was like a thunderclap. All sanity and coherence vanished in a maelstrom of red and silver-steel, a whirlpool, an avalanche of thrusting spears, speeding arrows, slashing blades. Elak was instantly surrounded by foes. His rapier flew swift as a striking snake; blood stained its length. His horse shrieked and fell hamstrung to the ground. Elak leaped free and saw Lycon charging to the rescue. The little man was wielding a sword almost as long as himself, but his pudgy fingers handled it with surprising ease. He lopped off one man's head, ruined another's face with a well-placed kick of his steel-shod foot, and then Elak had leaped astride a riderless steed.

Again he plunged into the fray. The brown bald head of Dalan was rising and falling some distance away; the druid roared like a beast as his sword whirled and flew and bit deep. Blood soaked the brown robe. Dalan's horse seemed like a creature possessed; it screamed shrilly blowing through red, inflamed nostrils, snapped viciously

103

and reared and struck with knife-edged hoofs. Druid and charger raged like a burning pestilence amid the battle; sweat and blood mingled on Dalan's toad face.

Elak caught sight of Sepher. The ruler of Kiriath, a bronzed bearded giant, towered above his men, fighting in deadly silence. Smiling wolfishly, Elak drove toward the king.

From the distance came the thin high wailing of pipes. Out of the side canyon men came pouring—barbarous man, half naked, their lean bodies smeared blue with woad. The men of Aynger! At their head ran Aynger himself, his gray beard flying, brandishing the hammer Helm-Breaker. The gray giant leaped upon a rock, gesturing toward the forces of Kiriath.

"Slay the oppressors!" he bellowed. "Slay! Slay!"

The weird pipes of the Amenalks shrilled their answer. The blue-painted men swept forward—

From the ranks of Sepher an arrow flew. It sped toward Aynger. It pierced his bare throat and drove deep—deep!

The Amenalk leader bellowed; his huge body arched like a bow. Blood spouted from his mouth.

A battalion charged out from the ranks of Kiriath. They sped toward the Amenalks, lances lowered, pennons flying.

Aynger fell! Dead, he toppled from the rock into the lifted arms of his men. The pipes skirled. The Amenalks, bearing their leader, turned and fled back into the valley!

Cursing, Elak dodged a shrewd thrust, killed his assailant, and spurred toward Sepher. The hilt of his rapier was slippery with blood. His body, under the chain-armor, was a mass of agonizing bruises; blood gushed from more than one wound. His breath rasped in his throat. The stench of sweat and gore choked him; he drove over ground carpeted with the writhing bodies of men and horses.

Down the valley Dalan fought and bellowed his rage. The battle-thunder crashed on the towering crags and sent deafening echoes through the Gateway.

Still the trumpets of Kiriath called; still the drums and cymbals of Cyrena shouted their defiance.

And still Sepher slew, coldly, remorselessly, his bronzed face expressionless.

Kiriath gathered itself and charged. The forces of Cyrena were forced back, fighting desperately each step of the way. Back to the narrowing of the pass they were driven.

High above the archers loosed death on Kiriath.

With ever-increasing speed Sepher's army thrust forward. A gust of panic touched the ranks of Cyrena. A dragon banner was captured and slashed into flying shreds by keen blades.

Vainly Elak strove to rally his men. Vainly the druid bellowed threats.

The retreat became a rout. Into the narrow defile the army fled, jammed into a struggling, fighting mob. An orderly retreat might have saved the day, for Kiriath could have been trapped in the narrow pass and crippled by boulders thrust down by the men stationed above. As it was, Cyrena was helpless, waiting to be slaughtered.

Kiriath charged.

Quite suddenly Elak heard a voice. In through the mountains. Above the call of trumpets came the thin wailing of pipes. Louder it grew, and louder.

From the side canyon the blue barbarians of Amenalk rushed in disorderly array. In their van a group ran together with lifted shields. Upon the shields was the body of Aynger!

Weirdly, eerily, the ear-piercing skirling of the pipes of Amenalk shrilled out. The woad-painted savages, mad with blood-frenzy, raced after the corpse of their ruler.

Dead Aynger led his men to war!

The Amenalks fell on the rear of the invaders. Flails and scythes and blades swung and glittered, and were lifted dripping red. A giant sprang upon the shield-platform, astride the body of Aynger. In his hand he brandished a war-hammer.

"Helm-Breaker!" he shouted. "Ho—Helm-Breaker!"

He leaped down; the great hammer rose and fell and slaughtered. Casques and helms shattered under the smashing blows; the Amenalk wielded Helm-Breaker in a circle of scarlet death about him.

*"Helm-Breaker! Ho—slay! Slay!"*

Kiriath swayed in confusion under the onslaught. In that breathing-space Elak and Dalan rallied their army. Cursing, yelling, brandishing steel, they whipped order out of chaos. Elak snatched a dragon banner from the dust, lifted it high.

He turned his horse's head down the valley. One hand lifting the standard, one gripping his bared rapier, he drove his spurs deep.

*"Ho, the Dragon!"* he shouted. *"Cyrena! Cyrena!"*

Down upon Kiriath he thundered. Behind him rode Lycon and the Druid. And after them the remnants of an army poured. Hira led his archers from the cliffs. The arbalasters came bounding like mountain goats, snatching up swords and spears, pouring afoot after their king.

*"Cyrena!"*

The drums and cymbals roared out again. Through the tumult pierced the thin, weird calling of the pipes.

*"Helm-Breaker! Slay! Slay!"*

And then madness—a hell of shouting, scarlet battle through which Elak charged, Dalan and Lycon beside him, riding straight for the bushy beard that marked Sepher. On and on, over screaming horses and dying men, through a whirlpool of flashing, thirsty steel, thrusting, stabbing, hacking—

The face of Sepher rose up before Elak.

The bronzed face of Kiriath's king was impassive; in his cold eyes dwelt something inhuman. Involuntarily an icy shudder racked Elak. As he paused momentarily, the brand of Sepher whirled up and fell shattering in a great blow.

Elak did not try to escape. He poised his rapier, flung himself forward in his stirrups, sent the sharp blade thrusting out.

The enchanted steel plunged into Sepher's throat. Simultaneously Elak felt his back go numb under the sword-cut; his armor tore raggedly. The blade dug deep into the body of the war-horse.

The light went out of Sepher's eyes. He remained for a heart-beat upright in his saddle. Then his face changed.

It darkened with swift corruption. It blackened and rotted before Elak's eyes. Death, so long held at bay, sprang like a crouching beast.

A foul and loathsome thing fell forward and tumbled from the saddle. It dropped to the bloody ground and lay motionless. Black ichor oozed out from the chinks of the armor; the face that stared up blindly at the sky was a frightful thing.

And without warning darkness and utter silence dropped down and shrouded Elak.

## 10. *The Black Vision*

And the devil that deceived them was cast into the lake of fire and brimstone, where are also the beast and the false prophet; and they shall be tormented day and night for ever and ever.

—Revelations 20:10

He felt again the dizzy vertigo that presaged the coming of Karkora. A high-pitched, droning whine rang shrilly in his ears; he felt a sense of swift movement. A picture came.

Once more he saw the giant crag that towered amid the mountains. The dark tower lifted from its summit. Elak was drawn forward; iron gates opened in the base of the pinnacle. They closed as he passed through.

The high whining had ceased. It was cimmerian dark. But in the gloom a Presence moved and stirred and was conscious of Elak.

The Pallid One sprang into view.

He felt a sense of whirling disorientation; his thoughts grew inchoate and confused. They were slipping away, spinning into the empty dark. In their place something crept and grew; a weird mental invasion took place. Power of Karkora surged through Elak's brain, forcing back the man's consciousness and soul, thrusting them out and back into the void. A dreamlike sense of unreality oppressed Elak.

Silently he called upon Dalan.

Dimly a golden flame flickered up, faraway. Elak heard the druid's voice whispering faintly, out of the abyss.

*"Mider—aid him, Mider—"*

Fires of Mider vanished. Elak felt again the sense of swift movement. He was lifted—

The darkness was gone. Gray light bathed him. He was, seemingly, in the tower on the summit of the crag —the citadel of Karkora. But the place was unearthly!

The planes and angles of the room in which Elak stood were warped and twisted insanely. Laws of matter and geometry seemed to have gone mad. Crawling curves swept obscenely in strange motion; there was no sense of perspective. The gray light was alive. It crept and shimmered. And the white shadow of Karkora blazed forth with chill and dreadful radiance.

Elak remembered the words of Mayana, the sea-witch, as she spoke of her monstrous son Karkora.

*"He walked in other worlds, beyond unlit seas, across the nighted voids beyond earth."*

Through the whirling chaos a face swam, inhuman, mad, and terrible. A man's face, indefinably bestialized and degraded, with a sparse white beard and glaring eyes. Again Elak recalled Mayana's mention of Erykion, the wizard who had created the Pallid One.

"Perhaps he dwells in his citadel yet, with Karkora. Not for years have I seen the sorcerer."

If this were Erykion, then he had fallen victim to his own creation. The warlock was insane. Froth dribbled on the straggling beard; the mind and soul had been drained from him.

He was swept back and vanished in the grinding maelstrom of the frightful lawless geometrical chaos. Elak's eyes ached as he stared, unable to stir a muscle. The shadow of the Pallid One gleamed whitely before him.

The planes and angles changed; pits and abysses opened before Elak. He looked through strange gateways. He saw other worlds, and with his flesh shrinking in cold horror he stared into the depths of the Nine Hells. Frightful life swayed into motion before his eyes. Things of inhuman shape rose out of nighted depths. A charnel wind choked him.

The sense of mental assault grew stronger; Elak felt his mind slipping away under the dread impact of alien power. Unmoving, deadly, Karkora watched—

"Mider," Elak prayed. "Mider—aid me!"

The mad planes swept about faster, in a frantic saraband of evil. The dark vision swept out, opening wider vistas before Elak. He saw unimaginable and blasphemous things, Dwellers in the outer dark, horrors beyond earth-life—

The white shadow of Karkora grew larger. The crawl-

109

ing radiance shimmered leprously. Elak's senses grew dulled; his body turned to ice. Nothing existed but the now gigantic silhouette of Karkora; the Pallid One reached icy fingers into Elak's brain.

The assault mounted like a rushing tide. There was no aid anywhere. There was only evil, and madness, and black, loathsome horror.

Quite suddenly Elak heard a voice. In it was the murmur of rippling waters. He knew Mayana spoke to him by strange magic.

"In your hour of need I bring you the talisman against my son Karkora."

The voice died; the thunder of the seas roared in Elak's ears. A green veil blotted out the mad, shifting planes and angles. In the emerald mists shadows floated—the shadows of Mayana.

They swept down upon him. Something was thrust into his hand—something warm and wet and slippery.

He lifted it, staring. He gripped a heart, bloody, throbbing—alive!

The heart of Mayana! The heart beneath which Karkora had slumbered in the womb! The talisman against Karkora!

A shrill droning rose suddenly to a skirling shriek of madness, tearing at Elak's ears, knifing through his brain. The bleeding heart in Elak's hand drew him forward. He took a slow step, another.

About him the gray light pulsed and waned; the white shadow of Karkora grew gigantic. The mad planes danced swiftly.

And then Elak was looking down at a pit on the edge of which he stood. Only in the depths of the deep hollow was the instability of the surrounding matter lacking. And below was a shapeless and flesh-colored hulk that lay inert ten feet down.

It was man-sized and naked. But it was not human.

The pulpy arms had grown to the sides; the legs had grown together. Not since birth had the thing moved by itself. It was blind, and had no mouth. Its head was a malformed grotesquerie of sheer horror.

Fat, deformed, utterly frightful, the body of Karkora rested in the pit.

The heart of Mayana seemed to tear itself from Elak's hand. Like a plummet it dripped, and fell upon the breast of the horror below.

A shuddering, wormlike motion shook Karkora. The monstrous body writhed and jerked.

From the bleeding heart blood crept out like a stain. It spread over the deformed horror. In a moment Karkora was no longer flesh-colored, but red as the molten sunset.

And, abruptly, there was nothing in the pit but a slowly widening pool of scarlet. The Pallid One had vanished.

Simultaneously the ground shook beneath Elak; he felt himself swept back. For a second he seemed to view the crag and tower from a distance, against the background of snow-tipped peaks.

The pinnacle swayed; the crag rocked. They crashed down in thunderous ruin.

Only a glimpse did Elak get; then the dark curtain blotted out his consciousness. He saw, dimly, a pale oval. It grew more distinct. And it was the face of Lycon bending above Elak, holding a brimming cup to the latter's lips.

"Drink!" he urged. "Drink deep!"

Elak obeyed, and then thrust the liquor away. He stood up weakly.

He was in the pass of the Gateway. Around him the men of Cyrena rested, with here and there a blue-painted warrior of Amenalk. Corpses littered the ground. Vultures were already circling against the blue.

Dalan was a few paces away, his shallow black eyes regarding Elak intently. He said, "Only one thing could have saved you in Karkora's stronghold. One thing—"

Elak said grimly, "It was given me. Karkora is slain."

A cruel smile touched the druid's lipless mouth. He whispered, "So may all enemies of Mider die."

Lycon broke in, "We've conquered, Elak. The army of Kiriath fled when you killed Sepher. And, gods, I'm thirsty!" He rescued the cup and drained it.

Elak did not answer. His wolf face was dark; in his eyes deep sorrow dwelt. He did not see the triumphant banners of the dragon tossing in the wind, nor did he envision the throne of Cyrena that waited. He was remembering a low, rippling voice that spoke with longing of the fields and hearth-fires of earth, a slim, inhuman hand that had reached through a curtain—a sea-witch who had died to save a world to which she had never belonged.

The shadow was lifted from Alantis; over Cyrena the golden dragon ruled under great Mider. But in a sunken city of marble beauty the shadows of Mayana would mourn for Poseidon's daughter.

*Thongor the Mighty is one of those legendary warrior heroes of the long dim past whose exploits are a part of the folk-myths our staider friends dismiss as sword-and-sorcery stories—ignoring the reality that it is only in our enlightened times that the Machine, and the Test Tube, have supplanted the Sword.*

# THIEVES OF ZANGABAL

## by Lin Carter

# THIEVES OF ZANGABAL

*Half a million years before the first pharaoh ruled beside the Nile or the first stone was laid in the foundations of Ur of the Chaldees, civilization arose in the savage, jungled wildernesses of ancient Lemuria, the Lost Continent of the Pacific. The greatest warrior of all that primal age was known as Thongor the Mighty, barbarian hero and wandering adventurer from the frozen wastes of the northlands, who warred and quested and battled his way across all that lost world of savagery and sorcery to the throne of man's first great civilization, the Golden Empire of the Sun. The saga of Thongor's rise to the Throne of the West has been told in a series of five novels: but here, for the first time in print, is the tale of one of his earliest adventures. It takes place eight months before the opening scenes of the first Thongor novel,* The Wizard of Lemuria, *in the Year of the Kingdoms of Man 7007, when Thongor was a young warrior of twenty-five.*

## 1. *In the Half of Seven Gods*

THE priest Kaman Thuu was old and gaunt and skeletal, his lean body wrapped in a robe of crimson velvet whereon the symbols of the Seven Gods of Zangabal were worked with stiff gold thread. Jeweled rings flashed and glittered on his clawed fingers, and his eyes burned keen and sharp in his shaven, skull-like head.

"We are agreed then," he purred. "For twenty pieces of gold you will rob the house of Athmar Phong the magician and fetch back to me the mirror of black glass you will find in his workshop. And this task you will fulfill this very night."

"Aye," the bronzed young giant grunted sourly, "but I like not the task."

"I have already explained that you have naught to fear at the hands of Athmar Phong," the priest reminded him silkenly. "This is the first day of Zamar, the first month of spring. On this night the magicians of the Grey Brotherhood to which Athmar Phong is sworn meet on a mountainous plateau far to the north of here for their vile and sorcerous sabbat. Thus will the magician be absent tonight, and thus you may thieve the mirror for us in utter safety."

"So you claim," the youth growled, "and so it may well be. But it is never wise to meddle in the affairs of wizards, and their houses go seldom unguarded. What if this Ptarthan sorceror has left behind a demon to watch over his treasures?"

Cold amusement flickered in the clever eyes of the gaunt priest. He ran his gaze over the broad shoulders, the long and powerfully muscled bare arms, and the deep, heavy-thewed chest of the young barbarian who sat before him in the veiled antechamber of the temple. And he

116

let his gaze linger on the massive hilt of the great two-handed Valkarthan broadsword that hung at the lean waist of the young thief in its long scabbard of dragon-leather.

"Surely you are not . . . *afraid?*" he suggested slyly.

The young barbarian flushed angrily. His strange gold eyes, that burned with sullen, wrathful fires under scowling black brows in his tanned face under the thick, unshorn mane of black hair, blazed with sudden temper. Then they cleared, and the youth threw back his head and laughed.

"Gorm!" he rumbled. "You sit here safe and secure in your silken nest, a pure and holy priest of the Gods of Zangabal who would never sully his sanctified fingertips with blood or crime—and pay another man to take risks and dare the perils you would shudder to face—and then taunt him with a hint of cowardice!" The burly young barbarian laughed again, and spat on the fine Pelorm carpet. "Wizards and priests! You are alike, the both of you—and I would have dealings with neither, if I had my way!"

The gaunt skull-face of Kaman Thuu tightened and his voice grew harsh and contemptuous. "Would you rather starve like a whining beggar in the back-alleys of Zangabal, barbarian? Because that you will do if you refuse the task I have set you. Remember, the Thieves' Guild is powerful in our city: to make your living as a thief here, you must join the Guild, or fight both your brother thieves and the city guard each time you attempt a robbery. And to enter the Guild, you must pay a heavy fee in gold. For weeks, by your own account, you have fought over scraps like a half-starved animal, stealing from the bazaar, lifting a fat purse, scrabbling like an *unza* for a bare subsistence. I alone have offered you gold for a task: reject my offer, and you perish miserably either of a starved belly or at the hands of the Guild—"

The young barbarian—his name was Thongor—waved away this cloud of words with a grunt of surly acknowledgement.

"I know all this, priest. And I also know why you come to me, an outlander, with your offer—because the self-respecting thieves of Zangabal have already rejected you! By Gorm the Father of Stars—even the cunning thieves of Zangabal dare not steal from this Ptarthan mage! But I must do it or starve, so save your breath. But I still ask: what if this Athmar Phong has left a demon to guard his house while he is absent? I have fought beasts and men ere now, but no warrior can pit naked steel against hellspawn and live!"

The priest narrowed thoughtful eyes.

"There is some truth in what you say, barbarian. Athmar Phong *is* reputed to hold a familiar spirit or elemental bound to his service. That is why we of the temple are willing to entrust to your hands a rare amulet which is one of our treasures."

He dipped one bony, bejeweled hand into his crimson robes and brought forth a small object of curious workmanship which he set gently on the tabletop between them, moving to one side the empty wine bottle and the remains of the meal of broiled *bouphar*-steak wherewith he had somewhat appeased the ravenous appetite of his surly guest.

The thing was as long as a man's middle finger and made of colorless crystal. It glittered in the orange light of the candelabra. Thongor picked it up gingerly, turning it so it caught the light. He scrutinized the amulet but could make nothing of it. The surface of the lucent crystal was engraved with a pattern of tiny hieroglyphics in some unknown language. He grunted sourly. A simple barbarian, bred in the savage wilderness of the frozen north, far from perfumed cities and silk-clad men, he had a healthy warrior's contempt for all this foul, sly witchery. Still, there was an odd glitter to the thing: and his fingers tingled with the faint currents of some uncanny force locked within the very structure of the crystal . . .

"What does this gewgaw do?" he rumbled mistrustfully.

"This amulet is called the Shield of Cathloda," the priest told him in a severe tone. "It is a rare protective amulet which diverts and absorbs the attack of magical forces, and it was made a thousand years ago in Zaar the Black City far to the east. It can rechannel or cancel anything up to ninth-order forces. Fear not; even if Athmar Phong has left magical traps or a guardian familiar of some kind, you will walk safely and unharmed."

Thongor studied the crystal cylinder for a few moments. Then he stood up, slipping the amulet into his pocket-pouch and drawing an immense hooded black cloak about his brawny shoulders.

"Very well, priest," he growled. "I will chance it for your gold . . . although something tells me it is a bargain I will yet live to regret—*if* I live!"


## 2. *Black Catacombs*


The priest thereupon led Thongor forth from the veiled antechamber and into the central nave of the colossal temple. At this hour of night there were no worshipers in the vast domed hall, which was murmurous with whispering echoes and filled with vague depths of gloom.

At the far end of the hall, which was lined with titanic pillars of pale marble that loomed up into the shadow-thronged darkness of the vault above like stone sequoias, stood towering idols hewn from seven kinds of stone: the Seven Gods they worshiped here in Zangabal on the Gulf.

Thongor eyed them grimly, unimpressed. The winged colossi, bearing mystic attributes and symbols in their many arms, tridents, stylized thunderbolts, crowns, swords, and less-recognizable accouterments, glared down at him, their stone faces shining in the dim gleam of coiling blue flames which glided heavenwards from a vast bronze bowl on the alabaster altar. The superstitions of the barbarian were bred deep in him, stamped deep in blood, brain and bone: but he knew them not, these alien godlings of the tropic, jungle-clad southlands: he swore only in the name of Father Gorm, the grim God-King of the dark northern wastes of ice and snow.

The priest led him around to the rear of the sevenfold dais whereon were upreared the stone colossi. There he touched a hidden catch. A panel of thick marble sank from view, soundless and sudden as a feat of magic, revealing the yawning mouth of a black cavern. Thongor growled, nape-hairs bristling at the thought of entering the ominous portal.

"This hidden route will carry you to the house of Athmar Phong," the priest said smoothly. "You will follow the yellow symbols only: they are shaped like the Yan Hu glyph—you know the characters of our southland language, do you not?"

"Aye," he nodded curtly.

"Then follow only the yellow Yan Hu, and it will lead you to the pits under the magician's house. Let me caution you not to stray from the path thus delineated, for other characters mark other routes, such as for example, the Shan Yom glyph, marked in red, which leads to the waterfront. You will come up beneath the house, and will thus avoid the many magical traps or defenses the Ptarthan wizard has doubtless set over his walls, his doors and his windows."

Despite the soothing words of the gaunt priest, the

brawny young warrior still hesitated at the threshold of the black tunnel's mouth.

"What are these cursed caverns—how came they here?" he demanded. "Since I bear your crystal toy, why should I not take my chances with the front gates and walk the streets under the open skies like a man? I am no skulking *unza*, to slink through your stinking sewers!"

The priest answered smoothly: "These cavernous passageways are very old; indeed, their origins are lost in the dim mists of the ancient past. But the chronicles of our temple tell that at the end of the Thousand-Year War with the fall of Nemedis in the east, the children of Nemedis came thither to found the nine cities of the west. It was Yaklar of the House of Ruz who was lord of the founding of Zangabal, and it is written that the hidden ways were here even ere the walls of the city were first raised. More than this we know not, but by means of this secret the temple is mighty in Zangabal, and even the Sark in his mighty palace is not beyond the reach of our eyes and ears, for the tunnels extend even under the royal precinct. But come, barbarian, you must linger no more: night passes swift-winged, and you must accomplish the theft of the black mirror ere dawn or be surprised in the midst of the task by the returning of Athmar Phong . . ."

The gaunt priest stood by the open portal until the grim-faced young warrior had vanished in the darkness of the tunnels; then he released the secret spring and closed the hidden door again.

He stood for a moment, fingering his lean jaw with bony fingers. With luck, the mirror would be in his possession before the first hour of morning, and with it— *power!* Power to bend even the strong will of Athmar Phong to his bidding. Power to command the secret of the mirror itself, by which he saw a clear path from this

121

place to a higher . . . to the throne of Zangabal itself! He smiled a slow, evil smile at the thought.

And, as for the barbarian—well, why should he squander even a portion of the gold his wiles had wrung from temple-worshipers? The youth could be disposed of without loss: he was not even a member of the Thieves' Guild, which was a stroke of good fortune, as the Guild took a disquieting degree of interest in the disappearance of its members. But no one would even miss the Outlander . . .

His hand went to the small glass phial concealed in a secret pocket of his robes. There was enough powder of that deadly narcotic called Rose-of-Dreams within the small phial to destroy a dozen such as Thongor of Valkarth . . .


Thongor strode through the darkness, his strange gold eyes questing about distrustfully and one hand at the hilt of his mighty broadsword. The cavernous passage was black as the depths of his savage northlander hell, and it reeked of dead things long unburied.

Dangling stalactites hung from the arched roof overhead, glistening wetly in the dim faint light. The very presence of the hanging spears of stone denoted the awesome and incredible age of these this network of secret passages beneath Zangabal, for Thongor understood that such were slowly built up over weary aeons of sluggish calcareous drippings. Almost he would have assumed the passages to be the work of nature from such evidence, but the walls and floors of the tunnels clearly showed the handiwork of the builder. For although obscured by centuries of neglect and decay, the ancient marks of stoneworking tools were still visible along his path. He wondered grimly what unknown people of earth's remotest dawn had built this subterranean ways, and for what mysterious purpose. Oft had he heard whispered myths of the pre-human Dragon Kings of lost and boreal Hyperborea, buried countless ages ago under the fathomless snows of the ultimate polar north. Legend told that the mystery-race of lost Hyperborea, sprung from the gliding serpent and not the jungle ape, as were the races of men, had ruled all of old Lemuria before the creation of Phondath the Firstborn, the Father of All Men. Could it have been the shadowy Hyperboreans who cut these passages through the depths of the world?

Shrugging, he put such questions aside. It were futile to puzzle over such mysteries, since he had no answer to the riddle. He strode forward, his black leather boots crushing the mold and pooled slime which bestrew the stony floor.

And then he came to the branching of the tunnel. One offshoot led away to his left, but it was marked with the Shan Yom symbol painted on the wall in strange pigments that glowed with cold crimson fires. The other passage, to his right, was emblazoned with the phosphorescent yellow glyph of Yan Hu. He took the right-hand way.

Cold water dripped from the roof above, slow drops splashing in black pools, beslimed and foul. Small sounds came to his ears as he strode forward: the squeak and scurry, the rattle of tiny claws rasping over wet stone; the tunnels were aswarm with *unza*, the hideous, naked scavanger-rodents of Lemuria. He could see the gemlike wink and glitter of small red eyes from the black mouths of side-tunnels as he moved forward. He ignored the scrabbling rats, but his hand tightened on the hilt of his broadsword: the *unza* are eaters-of-flesh, and where they slither thick may also be found larger and more dangerous creatures.

Once a black serpent slid across his path and he recoiled, choking back a curse. But the viper glided on, ignoring him even as he ignored the rats.

123

Once the foaming torrent of a subterranean river cut across his path. He crossed it by means of a narrow, arched bridge of stone. Icy spray splattered him from the black waters as they rushed by beneath his heels, and his feet slipped on the treacherous slimy mold with which the stone arch was crusted, but he plodded forward grimly.

He sullenly cursed the ironies of fate that had cast him up on this shore. Nine years had passed since he had found his way down across that mighty mountainous spine of the Lemurian continent, the Mountains of Mommur, from the frigid wastes of his homeland. As a boy of fifteen he had been the lone survivor of his clan, the Black Hawk people of Valkarth, who perished in a mighty battle with their sworn enemies, the Snow Bear tribe. The boy Thongor, armed with the mighty broadsword of Thumithar his sire, had cut his way through the cities of the south. He had been an assassin, a wandering adventurer, a thief—the last profession ending on the slave-galleys of Shembis from which he had escaped, leading a slave-mutiny and stealing the very galley whereon he had toiled under the overseer's singing whip.

Thence he had sailed south to Tarakus, the pirate city that lay at the foot of the Gulf of Patanga where it mingled with the wind-lashed waters of Yashengzeb Chun the Southern Sea. The youth had brawled and battled his way to power in the red roaring Kingdom of Corsairs: as one of the proud Captains of Tarakus he had swaggered through the narrow spray-swept streets of the little seaport draped in costly brocade, emeralds and rubies blazing about his corded throat, and the wealth of a dozen fat merchant ships piled in the basement of his great stone house. But, alas, his hot Valkarthan temper had been his doom, and he had slain the Pirate King in a duel still legended among the wild rogues of the Corsair Kingdom. He had fled with half the Tarakan navy at his heels, bearing off of his golden treasure-trove only the rags on his back and the mighty broadsword of his kingly sire. Thus, during the year past, he had fought his way through the jungled southland to the quays and docks of Zangabal, hoping to enter the Sark's service as a mercenary swordsman. But, that failing, he had fallen back on his old profession of thievery, and thus has come to the present perilous impasse—serving a black-hearted priest by robbing a dangerous and potent magician!

Suddenly a black wall swung up before his very face, and Thongor jerked his attention away from his wandering memories . . . his underground journey was over, and the house of Athmar Phong lay before him.

### 3. *Soft Lips*

Thongor ran his hands lightly, questing, over the wall of black stone that confronted him. The marked path ended here, that much was certain: behind this wall, then, must lie the pits below the house of the Ptarthan mage. But how to pass the wall?

Growling a curse on that smirking priest who had not forewarned him of this barrier, he fumbled about in the dark and at last—more by happy accident than by careful plan—his fingers found the hidden spring and depressed it. The smooth wall of black stone sank soundlessly into the earth and the warrior stepped forward into a gloom-drenched room cut from smooth heavy stone.

He did not, as of yet, seek to close the opening thus made. You can never be certain how swiftly you may wish to leave the house of a wizard, and a smart thief never closes a door behind him if he can help it.

The basement was piled with crates and bales and bar-

125

rels. Thongor did not waste time looking them over; he prowled through the darkness of the room, every sense at the alert, the great broadsword naked in his hand.

Soon he encountered a stone stair against the further wall, and followed it up to the next floor on silent feet. Pushing through a heavy hanging of purple cloth, he found himself in a room so weirdly furnished that at first all he could do was blink and stare and blink again as he stood in the doorway.

The walls were of smooth stone faced with gray plaster and lined with shelves of dark wood. Along these were stacked and piled a jumble of curious things. Bottles and jars and flasks filled with colored liquids and nameless powders, bundles of dry withered leaves and grotesquely shapen roots, little cloth bags tied with a drawstring and filled, perhaps, with strange drugs and deadly powders.

And books—more of these than Thongor had ever seen before! Huge, thick, ponderous tomes made of crinkly sheets of rough parchment crudely bound in heavy leather or carven wood or painted ivory panels.

This, he knew, must be the magical workshop of Athmar Phong. A massive desk of oily black wood, carven all over with grinning devil-masks, stood to one end of the room, its top littered with hieroglyphic charts and curious instruments of brass and crystal. A man's skull of browned bone stood as a paperweight on one corner of the desk, and rubies were set in the sockets of the skull-like eyes. They glinted with malign small lights that seemed to follow his movement as he crossed the room.

A monstrous stuffed dragon-hawk, a winged and terrible flying dragon, hung from wires suspended from the rafters.

In a globe filled with milky fluid, a human brain floated.

Thongor noticed that this room was well lit, although he could not discover the source of the illumination. Gazing about, he could see no windows, neither were there any lamps or candles or torches to be seen: nevertheless the chamber was bathed in a harsh, gray, sterile light that leached most of the color out of things. A prickle of unease crawled down his spine, and, as he could not see the black mirror the priest had sent him here to fetch, he hastily quitted the silent room and pushed through a velvet-hung doorway into an adjoining chamber.

Whereas the first room had been cold and grim and workmanlike, with its harsh gray illumination and bare stone floors, this second chamber was a nest of silken luxury. The air reeked with heavy perfumes from a fat silver incense-lamp on a low tabouret of sleek blond wood inlaid with small panels of delicate ivory, exquisitely sculptured with shockingly detailed pornographic tableaus. A long, low divan lay along the further wall—and there, languorously coiled amidst a nest of bright-colored fat cushions, a young girl of breathtaking loveliness watched him from dark almond eyes.

The shock of discovering that the room was occupied by another stunned Thongor for an instant—but no longer. The hair-trigger reflexes of a barbarian warrior took over. The keen point of the great broadsword came up and hovered a half-inch from the base of the girl's throat.

"One sound—one word—!" Thongor growled.

The girl smiled slightly, and continued to regard him from under thick sooty lashes. Thongor looked her over curiously. She could have been eighteen, but no older, for her sleek soft body was as slim and graceful as a young panther. A thin sheet of green silk was drawn partly across her white body, leaving bare one arm and one long slender leg, with a silver disc upon the tip of each of her young breasts. Her long thick hair was fire-red with gold gleams shot through and through the silken tresses. Thongor had never seen a redheaded girl

127

before, but he knew that some of the slave women in the harems of the southland kings used color dyes, which may have explained the dazzling shade of her tresses, which were woven into one thick braid with strands of glowing pearls.

Her face was filled with fresh young beauty. Dark, tip-tilted eyes under thick black lashes, a full-lipped warmly crimson mouth; and soft delicate skin of flawless pallor.

"Thank the Gods you have come!" the girl breathed in a low, quiet voice, deep and husky. She writhed a little on the silken divan, and the thin covering of green silk slipped awry a trifle, revealing the naked curve of her thigh and a slim hip. Slowly, so as not to trigger him into action, the girl lifted into view her slim bare arms: they were bound at the wrist with manacles made of small gold chains.

"Who are you, lass? The wizard's concubine?" he demanded roughly, still holding the great sword at her warm throat.

"The wizard's slave . . ." she sighed. Then, before he could speak, she continued in a rush of words: "Athmar Phong stole me from my people when I was eleven; for seven hideous years I have been his helpless slave, the subject of every vile whim and loathsome fancy that came into his black, putrid heart!" Her shallow young breasts rose and fell, straining the green silk of her covering taut with every breath.

"For seven years I have dreamed and prayed that some-one would come to free me from this hideous bondage . . . and at last *you* have come to break my chains and set me free!"

Heedless of his lifted sword, the girl slid from the couch and knelt before Thongor, the heart shaped oval of her face lifted to him, tears trembling on her sooty lashes.

"Free me . . . free me, warrior . . . and I will gladly be *your* slave!" she whispered.

Thongor was young, and he had been without a woman since leaving Tarakus a year before, so it is not surprising that the blood rose hotly within him. Growling a calming word or two, he sheathed his sword and bent to snap the slender golden chains that bound the wrists of the helpless girl. Then he lifted her from her knees in his strong arms. She curled languorously against him, her slim arms sliding around his waist, her naked legs smooth and soft against his bare thighs. The pulse thundered in his temples as he felt the resilient warmth of her breasts pressing against his bare chest through the thin silk covering that was all she wore. She lifted her soft, trembling mouth to his lips. Another instant and he might well have forgotten the dangers of this place, and the perilous mission that had brought him . . . another instant and he might have lost himself in the warm softness of her . . .

But even as her panting kiss seared his mouth, even as his brawny arms encircled her slim hips, one sly hand slipped into his pocket-pouch—and the girl sprang halfway across the room and turned to laugh mockingly at him—with the Shield of Cathloda clenched between her slim white fingers!

## 4. *Spawn of Hell*

For a moment he stood frozen with shock, his senses still tingling with the warmth and softness of her slim young body. She stood across the room, her lips parted —and laughed.

But not the soft laughter of a young girl! Peal after ringing peal of hideous metallic mirth boomed and

129

roared from her soft warm lips—and even as he stared uncomprehendingly, dazed with the swiftness of the change—hellish fires blazed up in her almond eyes. They flamed like pits of burning sulfur! And now that she laughed, her lips were drawn back, revealing hideous yellow tusks, like those in the black, blubbery, bristling jaws of the savage Lemurian jungle boar.

She began to . . . *change*.

Her limbs blurred, then grew transparent as smoke, then remolded themselves. A ghastly parrot-beak thrust from the warm oval of the girl's face. Blazing orbs of yellow fire seethed with hellish mockery beneath her arched brows. Her hands became scaly bird-claws, armed with ferocious talons.

"Fool of a mortal," the bird-demon croaked in a ringing metallic voice, "I knew of your presence within the house of my master from the first moment you set foot herein, and I chose a form that would lull your suspicions—"

Thongor struck!

The girl-thing had befooled him for a few moments —but now the fighting instincts of a northlands warrior turned him into a battling engine of destruction! One hand flashed out, scooped up the fat round silver incense-lamp and hurled it straight as an arrow into the demon's half-transformed face. The thud of heavy silver against flesh was audible the length of the room. The monster, its body still a hideous blend of exquisite human female and grisly bird-thing, staggered back from the impact.

The silver lamp broke open, and glowing pink coals splattered the half-changed body of the demon guardian! In an instant, the disarranged piece of green silk the devil still wore went up in a flash of flame. Blazing coals dribbled down between the white soft breasts of the girl-like torso, raising terrible weals and blisters. The parrot-beak gaped open, screeching with agony and fury.

Thongor had not paused, as would a civilized man of the southern cities, to use reason; instinct alone told him that if the demon still wore flesh, that flesh could feel pain!

He followed the flying brazier with the small tabouret on which it had stood. This he hurled like a powerful catapult straight at the ghastly scaled claw that clutched the protective talisman. The blunt edge of the wooden tabouret caught the slim girl's wrist, which had only partly changed into demon's claw. The bone snapped with the sound of a dry branch cracking. The claw sagged limply as the demon howled—and the amulet fell!

Thongor dove across the room. His flying body crashed against the tender girl-legs of the monster and sent it reeling back against the further wall, while he scooped out one hand to catch the talisman. Luckily the fragile crystal thing had fallen on thick, soft carpets —had the floor been of bare stone, like the workshop through which he had recently passed, his only hope of escaping from this den of hell alive would have smashed to a thousand tiny shards.

Swift as he was, the demon was swifter. Even as he went crashing back against the wall, it—*changed*. The body crumbled into a coiling length of smoky stuff, and one arm snaked out, inhumanly long, to snatch the fallen amulet almost out of Thongor's very fingers.

The young warrior came to his feet in a rush, steel singing as he tore his sword from its scabbard.

The demon melted before him, reassembling itself across the room. Only the hand which grasped the all-important amulet had remained solid on this plane as the demon moved. Thongor took a swipe at it, but missed.

Now he lunged for the monster, swinging up the mighty broadsword, deep chest thundering forth his primitive challenge. The great sword swung glittering

131

up and came hissing down to clang against the scaled, reptilian body of the demon, by now fully transformed to its normal appearance on the earth-plane.

It was like swinging at a wall of solid steel! The shock traveled up Thongor's arms to the shoulders, numbing and paralyzing even his mighty thews. The demon's breast was solid as iron. It was astonishing that the blade of the sword did not shiver to fragments from the impact. But they had wrought well, those wonder-smiths of age-old Nemedis from which the ancient sword had come: potent spells and powerful runes had filled the crystalline structure of the great steel sword with terrific power. The blade held, although nicked: but the ringing shock numbed Thongor to the shoulder and the great sword fell from his nerveless fingers to clang like a stricken bell against the stone floor that lay beneath the carpets.

His arms temporarily helpless, Thongor lashed out with a booted foot. Howling with harsh mockery, the great yellow beak of the demon was open, and Thongor's booted foot crashed into its mouth, crushing the beak to gory ruin! Green hell-blood spurted from the crushed face of the devil, and again it went reeling back against the wall.

Thongor began to understand the limitations of the thing. It had complete control over its body and could doubtless transform itself to the likeness of any creature in earth, hell or heaven, but it was slow of thought. Anticipating a blow from the great Valkarthan broadsword, it had increased the density of the matter whereof its breast was composed until it reached the hardness of solid metal—but had not thought to extend the same protection to the rest of its body!

Thus, if the young barbarian could keep it off balance, he might yet defeat the creature, or at least wrest the powerful talisman from its clutches. He dove after

132

the monster as it fell squalling to the floor, its face a bubbling gory wreck.

He landed squarely upon it, both booted feet crashing down in its groin with crippling weight.

It was naked now, the green silk covering of its girlguise burnt away by the scattering coals, and sexless as a stone to the eye, at least, but still vulnerable to such a brutal blow. He came crashing down with both feet and heard it voice a shrill shriek of bestial agony. Alien organs crunched and popped under his weight, and more of the green gore splattered from pulped flesh.

But it availed him little. For a second only it squalled and flopped in pain—then it hardened its body to the density of steel all over. He could feel it happening even as he grappled with the wriggling thing.

They were both on their feet in a moment, battling lustily. Thongor swung balled fists into the thing's gut and groin, but only tore the skin from his brawny knuckles and numbed his hands again. He shouldered it with terrific force, hoping to break free, and for a moment he took the monster-thing by surprise and shoved it off-balance. He heard bird-clawed feet rip through the soft carpeting and squeak against naked stone as it fought to regain its balance.

Then two great hands like twin iron vises closed about his throat and—*squeezed*.

Blood roared in Thongor's ears like pounding surf. A red haze thickened before his eyes, obscuring his vision. Dimly he could see the snarling visage of the demon's beaked face—now repaired and whole—screeching into his own. But the crushing and intolerable pressure on his throat sent needles of unbearable torment lancing through and through his brain like thrusts of pure blinding flame.

He fought desperately with every atom of strength in all his mighty form. Lashing out with strong legs, he sought to crush the clawed feet of his foe or entangle his legs and knock him off balance, but to no avail. The demon increased the density of its body, and thus its weight, till it stood as unmovable as a pyramid of solid stone. Thongor rammed his burly shoulders into its chest, thudded balled fists into midsection and groin—but again, to no avail.

He could not breathe. The iron strength of the howling brute was crushing the very life out of him. Strength drained from his knees; he sagged toward the floor, still battling like a titan. His vision had darkened now, so that he could hardly see. He knew his face must be black from congested blood, a snarling tiger-mask of grim ferocity. The blood roared in his ears like a thousand seas plunging over the edges of the world to shatter like a thunderclap against the foundations of eternity.

He fought on, as consciousness ebbed and darkness closed around him like black rising waters.

He passed into utter blackness, still fighting . . .

## 5. Ald Turmis

Thongor came awake like some great jungle cat. His savage heritage had honed his reflexes to exquisite keenness. He did not come awake through slow, foggy transitional stages, as softer city-bred men awaken, but all at once—from total unconsciousness to full, tingling alertness, like a jungle predator whose slumbers are disturbed by the faint, distant snapping of a twig.

A dim remote light beat about him.

Cold, rough, wet stone was against his naked back and his numb wrists were stretched against the wall of rock, clamped helpless with thick bands of icy metal.

He was in a large, empty chamber cut from naked stone. This his hearing told him instantly; he could hear the faint echoes of water dripping down through the foundations of the building above. From the darkness, the moisture, the foul stench, he reasoned that he must be in some dungeon cell beneath the house of the Ptarthan wizard. His cloak was gone, his sword and other weapons and accouterments—even the pocket-pouch at his waist, where a few lonely coins were stored against hunger.

But these things mattered little. He was surprised to find himself still alive!

And alive he was, or all the myths were wrong—for surely no disembodied spirit could feel such pain as went throbbing and pulsing from every nerve in his body. He took a deep breath, and felt the red waves of pain beating against the very citadel of his mind. His body felt as if every inch of it had been beaten all over with leather clubs. But he still lived.

"I wasn't sure whether you were alive or not," drawled a young man's lazy voice very close to him. Thongor felt the icy drench of shock go through him, and twisted his head about—ignoring the blaze of pain from sore, bruised muscles—to find he had a cell-mate.

His companion was a slim dark young man, Thongor's age or perhaps a year or two younger, who wore the simple red leather harness of a lone fighting-man unattached to the service of any house or lord. The young wore a scruffy beard of perhaps two weeks' growth, and was somewhat soiled and stained from the filthy dungeon.

Thongor took him in in one swift, measuring glance. The young man was well bred, with intelligent dark eyes and a not-unpleasant smile, if a trifle dispirited and sardonic, and he had about him the trim, supple, hard-muscled look of a good fighting-man.

Thongor relaxed, grunting.

"I live," he said simply. "Why are you not bound, as I am?" he asked immediately, for his companion was secured by a single chain about his booted leg which was fastened to a ring set in the wall.

The young man grinned faintly. "Because Athmar Phong's pet devil had no trouble in knocking me witless, in contrast to the battle *you* put up. I gather he doesn't consider me of any particular danger. Unlike you—he must judge you a worthy opponent, even for a demon. I could hear the fight all the way down here: it must have been a magnificent brawl!"

"It was," Thongor grunted, "but I lost it. Who are you, and why are you here?"

The dark youth cocked a quizzical brow. "For that matter— I might ask the same of you, my friend!"

The barbarian grinned. "Be it so: I am Thongor, a warrior out of Valkarth in the northlands. I sought to steal a magic mirror from this Ptarthan sorcerer, but it seems I have yet a few things to learn about the profession of thievery. And you?"

His companion smiled wryly. "I am named Ald Turmis, and my city is Zangabal. *Belarba*," he said, and Thongor returned the familiar Lemurian word of greeting. The dark young Thurdan regarded him closely.

"Our sanitary facilities are somewhat limited, but I used most of what water we have to clean you up a bit," he said. "There is still a little, if you thirst."

"I thirst; but also, I hunger," Thongor admitted. "I don't suppose there is any—wine?"

Ald Turmis laughed. "A man who has just escaped alive from a barehanded battle with a demon deserves wine aplenty! Alas, we have none. But there is a jug of ale, and some meat."

Since the barbarian was bound in such a way he could not use his hands, Ald Turmis had to help him eat and drink. Thongor downed the strong, sour ale in great gulps, and felt his head clear and new life spread through his battered body. The meat was cold and dry and tough, but it was meat; he ate until his hunger was appeased, then he lay back with a grunt of contentment. With a full belly, a man could face the future on its own terms.

Ald Turmis had been looking thoughtful. At last, when the barbarian had eaten, he spoke up.

"I don't suppose," he began carefully, "that it was a certain Zangabali priest named Kaman Thuu who hired you to rob this house . . ."

Thongor blinked. "How did you know?"

Ald Turmis shrugged. "I, too, am down on my luck, Valkarthan. I have been traveling about the cities of the Gulf, seeking a place to sell my sword. I should have gone to Thurdis, it seems, for the new Sark of that city, Phal Thurid by name, has ambitions of conquest and empire and is hiring an enormous mercenary army. But, at any rate, I have thus far failed to find a sine-cure, and turned to thievery. This same Kaman Thuu offered me gold to steal a certain mirror from the house of Athmar Phong. That was half-a-moon ago, and I have been languishing in this cell ever since . . ."

"Gorm's Blood!" Thongor rumbled. "That sneaking pig of a priest! He didn't tell me there had been others!"

Ald Turmis smiled narrowly. "If he had, you might not have followed his wishes."

"There is truth in that," the barbarian growled. "Why does he seek so diligently for this cursed mirror? 'Tis not a wench's vanity, that's sure; he is as ugly as a skull."

"Oh, but it is a very famous mirror—the mirror of Zaf-far, as 'tis called. He was a mighty wizard of Patanga in ancient days, and this magic glass holds therein imprisoned a great Demon Prince, who must obey him who holds the Zaffar's mirror. All the secrets of time and space, all the wisdom of past ages, all the cryptic lore of age-lost and legended Hyperborea is his who possesses the mighty

137

mirror. Doubtless our priestly friend seeks power, as was ever the way of priests . . ."

Thongor's gold eyes blazed under black, scowling brows. They burned amberous and fiery as the eyes of lions.

"Well, if ever I get free of these chains, I will smash his cursed mirror over his shaven pate for not giving me warning I was walking into a trap," he growled.

## 6. Naked Steel

For a time they slept, the two of them, their talk done. Food and drink and rest did much to restore the animal strength of Thongor's battered body. When he awoke again, rested and refreshed, he tugged at his bonds restlessly.

"Enough of snoring our time away," he rumbled, nudging Ald Turmis to wakefulness with one foot. "This Ptarthan mage will return hither with dawn. It must be near that now, an hour or so hence, perhaps. If we are ever to free ourselves we must do it soon, for once the wizard has us in his grasp we are doomed men. Naked steel cannot battle against blasts of magic."

"We are already doomed men," Ald Turmis yawned. "For bare hands cannot battle naked steel, and I have long since given up trying to break my chains."

"But I have not yet tried," Thongor said quietly, and there was something in the level quality of his voice that made Ald Turmis feel a thrill of hope.

"You have the body of a gladiator, Thongor, and the thews of a god. But surely even you cannot burst our chains?"

There was a note of question in his voice, but Thongor merely grunted and turned to examine his bonds. His arms were spread against the stone wall at his back, and his wrists were held flat against the wall by bands of iron riveted to the stone. The position was cleverly thought out: thus bound he could only employ a portion of his strength towards freeing himself, and could use little if any leverage. Still, a man can try.

He took deep breaths, his massive chest swelling with power. Great ropes of sinewy muscle writhed across his naked shoulders and down his mighty arms. He set his back firmly against the wet, rough stone, and strove against the bonds. Although his face blackened with effort and the thews of his torso hardened like solid rock, the bonds gave not. He relaxed, breathing deeply; then he threw every ounce of surging strength in his terrific body against the bonds once more. Ald Turmis watched with growing fascination. The primal, brute strength of this half-naked barbarian was something beyond his experience.

City-bred men are for the most part shielded against the raw world of nature—for this is the purpose of cities. Raised behind walls, guarded by armies, they but rarely are forced to pit their naked strength against the savage wild.

But Thongor was born on the wintry steppes of the most terrible wilderness on all the earth. The child of wandering hunters, born to bare rock and numb snow and howling winds, in a cruel land surrounded with merciless enemies, men, beasts, and the hostile forces of nature, he was driven to battle for survival almost from the very hour of his birth. At an age when most boy-children can scarcely walk, Thongor had fought with his brothers against hungry wolves, knee-deep in frozen snow, with only a piece of rock for a weapon. Hunting the great white bear of the north, he had lived for days alone on the mighty glaciers with no nourishment but the hot blood of his kill to sustain him. The struggle for survival in

139

the savage wilderness is brutal and fierce; the weak die swift, and only the mightiest of men survive. Thongor had survived the cold, the harsh winds, the ferocious competition, and the cruel years of his boyhood had driven the hard iron of barbarian manhood deep within him.

The iron band—*broke!*

Like twin shadows, Thongor and Ald Turmis prowled through the darkness of the secret passage within the walls of the wizard's house on silent feet. They went armed with lengths of chain, since both the great Valkarthan broadsword and the Zangabali's slim rapier had been wrested from them when they were captured. But a length of iron chain is better than no weapon at all, and in this dark house of magic and mystery a man needed a weapon in his hands.

Privately, Ald Turmis thought they were fools not to flee when they had the chance. But Thongor could be grimly stubborn: he sought his great sword, and would not leave without it.

It had been comparatively easy, with one shackle broken and one arm freed, to break loose of the other. Then, with his bare fingers, the mighty Valkarthan had pried open a link of the chain that bound Ald Turmis to the ring set in the wall. Arming themselves with lengths of the very chains that had bound them, the two young warriors stole silently from their cell and into the depths of the cellars of the house. Their first thought had naturally been of escape, for the concealed door to the network of underground tunnels still lay open. But soon they had discovered the tunnels extended directly into a secret passage within the very walls of the house itself, as well as into the basements. Thus the Valkarthan had refused to flee like a thief in the night, and insisted they use this rare opportunity to recover their weapons, at least. Ald Turmis had argued, but to no avail. To the civilized Zangabali, his sword was little more than a tool, and easily replaced. But to the grim barbarian, the mighty broadsword was like a part of his body: he had lived with it by his side too long to abandon it now through fear.

The wizard's house had many rooms and many floors. Cleverly concealed eye-holes, hidden among the wall-decorations, permitted them to spy on the contents of these chambers.

The first room they inspected in this manner was a laboratory given over to alchemy. A great stone fireplace covered most of one wall, and upon its hearth a magic fire of yellow and purple flames crackled, heating the simmering contents of strange glass spheres. A profusion of chemical equipment cluttered long low tables of porcelain and steel. Glass and ceramic containers of bewildering design bore colored fluids of unguessable nature. And strange instruments of the alchemic science loomed in the wavering, twi-colored light of the mystic fire: crucibles and athanors, curcubits and aludels, and all manner of peculiar devices beyond their knowledge even to name.

The next room was given over to an even more terrible purpose. Herein stood huge vats of milky crystal, filled with thick soupy fluids. Naked bodies lay within immersed in the cloudy depths of these vats. They could not tell if these were the bodies of human beings or of animals—all they could see was the gleam of pallid flesh. But Thongor guessed the loathsome purpose of the equipment, and his shackles rose along his nape.

"Breeding vats!" he growled. "Look against the farther wall!"

And indeed it seemed that the Ptarthan wizard was engaged in the ultimate blasphemy itself, the attempt to duplicate the miracle of life. For steel-barred cages ran the length of the further wall, and therein resided the grisly

141

results of the wizard's experiments, or those of them which had gone awry. After one fascinated look, Ald Turmis spat a heart-felt curse and turned his eyes away from the hideous, deformed hybrids that wriggled, slithered and mewled behind the steel bars. There was one creature whose pink, glistening body was almost covered with eyes . . . eyes that wept with unutterable sadness, as if the thing had brain and wit enough to realize its own loathsomeness.

Another was a horrible blending of naked young girl and monster plant. Her bare body glistened wetly, pallid and unhealthy, although beautifully and perfectly formed. But her wrists and ankles ended in hairy thick roots, and her bald head was faceless—a thick profusion of pink, fleshy flower-petals.

"By the Nineteen Gods," Ald Turmis cursed sickly, "why does he let the pitiful things live—they should be put out of their misery with clean steel, and burnt!"

"Come," Thongor growled, "there are other rooms." They went on and came to a chamber whose walls were hung with silken hangings that rippled with black and crimson like leaping flames. From the vast, complex pentacle traced with glowing chalks against a floor of black marble, the nature of this third chamber was easy to guess. They needed not the stench of brimstone that permeated the air, to know that this room was given over to the wizard's conjurations. Here he performed those forbidden rituals whereby one might summon up demons from below or spirits from beyond. The very air tingled with unholy magic. They passed on, hurriedly.

Many other rooms were thus inspected, and they saw these were given over to wizardly arts almost beyond conjecture.

One there was that was completely lined with mirrors. Walls, ceiling and floor were one vast glittering sheet of reflecting glass. Mirrored wall reflected mirrored wall

142

and thus on into infinity. The purpose of this mysterious chamber was beyond the comprehension of the two swordsmen, but something about the room as unsettling. It was as if space itself was twisted and distorted among those endlessly reflecting, self-mirroring walls. They caught a weird glimpse of an endless nothingness that lay beyond the strictures of space . . . yawning gulfs of glittering emptiness stretched away forever.

From this terrible glimpse into the abyss they tore their gaze with difficulty. The echoing vastnesses of dim shadowy light caught and held their attention with a fascination almost hypnotic.

In this room of mirrors, a man could lose himself, could become forever lost in rapt contemplation of endless infinity, his mind wandered trapped and helpless between glittering planes of nothingness . . .

They came at last to the central hall of the wizard's house, and Thongor stifled a grunt of satisfaction. A stone dais of many steps supported a sparkling crystal throne, and there on the topmost step lay their two swords.

"Come!" he grunted, questing fingers questing for the spring that would release the secret door. The hall was untenanted; the guardian demon nowhere in sight. The door slid open noiselessly and they stepped forth into the hall.

*And the demon laughed!*

## 7. *Swords against Sorcery*

The hall was broad and high. Stone columns worked with weird runes and glyphs rose to support a cupola of scarlet crystal high overhead. A floor of polished stone tile rang underfoot. Tall stands of glittering brass held up enormous branching candles of perfumed wax which cast a wavering gold light over the dark emptiness of the wizard's seat of power. Hangings wrought of curious fabrics, depicting nightmarish visions drawn from ultimate chaos, hung between the columns; in the flickering light, distorted demoniac figures leered and grimaced and beckoned from these tapestries with the illusion of life.

But Thongor spared but a swift, all-encompassing glance on the decor. He spun to confront the devil-guardian whose mocking laughter pealed through the vaulted hall in a thunder of echoes.

"There!" Ald Turmis yelled hoarsely.

Thongor turned, iron chains swinging in his hands. The demon had fooled them by rendering itself invisible to sight. Now it melted into being atop the dais whereon towered the sparkling crystal throne of its master.

Seven feet tall it stood, bestraddling their swords, which were laid at the foot of the throne like an offering. The heart of Thongor grew cold at the appearance of the thing. Now it had taken on its normal form for this plane—a scaled and reptilian thing with a bird's beak and hooked claws. A jagged scarlet crest adorned its flat, blunt, triangular skull, and a serpent's tail lashed the sone steps. Burning eyes blazed sulfurously down at them with cruel triumph.

"Foolish mortals, not to flee when you had the chance!" it roared in a brazen voice. "For now you perish! I had hoped to spare you for my master's pleasure, but now —*die!*"

Thongor crouched, knees bent, the chain swinging loosely, ready for whatever might occur. Ald Turmis backed across the hall towards one of the tall, towering brass candelabra as the demon launched itself at Thongor.

It sprang like a dragon-cat of the jungle, claws bared

and glittering in the fiery light. But in the very middle of its incredible leap, it *changed*. A sheet of flame enveloped the hurtling form, and it shrunk into a ball.

The globe of flame hurled directly toward Thongor.

At the last possible moment, the barbarian leaped aside with a lithe tigerish bound. The globe of fire flashed through the space where he had stood a half-second before.

And, as he leaped aside, Thongor swung the heavy iron chain with all the strength in his mighty arms and shoulders. The heavy iron links whistled through the air and caught the flaming sphere a terrific blow.

Thongor had learned something of the demon's nature. While its powers were great, the limitations that were imposed upon it by nature on this plane gave him a certain degree of hope. True, its ability to change shape and substance was Protean—but while in any specific form it was bound by the natural limitations of that form.

For example, as a flying globe of flame the thing was virtually substanceless, light and flimsy. It could not have, simultaneously, the lightness of flying fire and the iron-hard density of its bird-devil form.

Hence the smashing blow of the heavy iron chain burst the burning globe into a shower of flying fragments. Bits of flame splattered over the floor. Of course, the demon could re-form—but that would take a few seconds of time.

Thongor seized that momentary advantage. In three lithe bounds he had cleared the steps of the dais, snatched up his mighty sword and tossed the slim rapier to Ald Turmis.

Rivulets of flame snaked over the floor and merged into a burning globe again. But now Thongor was doubly armed: the great broadsword was clenched in his right hand and the heavy length of iron chain dangled

145

from his left. He was ready to pit himself against the demon now—as ready as he would ever be. If it came at him in its fire form again, he would again smash it to flying sparks.

But the seething sphere of flames darkened, blurred. It became a monstrous shadowy form that congealed and hardened. Birdlike wings branched from hunched shoulders, but they were wings of steel! The neck elongated and a long beak pointed thrust forth. The demon shaped itself into the likeness of a fantastic bird of metal. The feathers that clad its form and its mighty wings were hard, cold metal, like dagger blades! The long beak thrust forth like a spearpoint. Clad in glittering metal, the bird-thing rose into the air and sailed at Thongor where he stood atop the dais. Wings of glistening steel beat clangorously, heavily, but they supported the clumsy monster aloft. And Thongor's blade and chain would prove feeble weapons against the steel-clad flying monster—

Then, unexpectedly, Ald Turmis struck. The demon, whose intelligence was limited, had almost forgotten his presence. Concentrating on its primary foe, the giant barbarian it had neglected to attend to the young Zangabali swordsman who stood in the shadows of the column-lined wall.

The youth turned and seized up the heavy brass candle abrum. Seven feet in the air it loomed, and it was heavy as a man—but desperation lent Ald Turmis new strength, and with a mighty heave he tugged it up and hurled it square against the steel bird as it lurched heavily in flight.

The crashing weight of the massive brass stand brought the steel bird down. It clanged thunderously against the marble pave, and the steel-sheathed wings cracked! The long serpentine neck broke and the spear-beaked head went rolling and clattering across the tiles.

146

"Well thrown!" Thongor boomed.

Ald Turmis flashed a grin and sprang from his place by the wall to snatch up the severed head. Perhaps he had some wild hope of preventing the demon from reforming somehow. If so, the hellish powers of the monsters were too swift for him.

The heavy cold metal of the head melted into smoke in his very hands. A cloud of green vapor leaked through his clutching fingers and floated across the floor. The broken bird of steel now collapsed into a swirling mass of emerald smoke into which the head-portion mixed and mingled.

A bodiless streamer of dense green vapor, the demon rose. It floated through the air like a cloud of smoke borne by the gusts of the wind.

Straight for the place where Thongor stood astride the high dais it drifted . . . to settle about his throat!

## 8. *The Shield of Cathloda*

As the smoke-serpent floated towards him, Thongor struck. His great broad sword swung through the vaporous body of the thing but harmed it not. The drifting banner of vapor was momently broken by the passage of his sword blade, but it melted together almost instantly.

It swirled about him, and for a moment he was hidden in the cloud of green smoke. Then two vaporish tendrils uncoiled from the mass and lashed about the throat of the young warrior. As the clammy fingers of vapor touched his flesh they congealed—hardened—took on weight and density.

Slithering tentacles of tough leathery flesh tightened in a stranglehold, cutting off his air.

Thongor's weapons clanged against the steps of the

147

dais as he snatched at the tightening tentacles of the smoke-thing. His iron fingers tugged to loosen the crushing coils. Green vapor seethed about him. Starved for air, his lungs strained, his mighty chest heaved.

The sinuous tentacles sank into his flesh with incredible strength. He fought on, as more and more portions of the green cloud solidified into slithering tendrils which slapped into place about his struggling form. One curled about his narrow waist, squeezing with a crushing grip. Another lashed about one booted foot, seizing a firm hold, and then snaked out and coiled around his other leg—and tightened, toppling him off balance and sending him crashing against the top of the dais.

Ald Turmis came yelling across the room, brandishing his slim rapier, to aid him in his threshing struggle against the kraken-form. But before the gallant young Zangabali could spring to the aid of his embattled comrade, chance, or fate, intervened.

Thrashing about, striving for a firm hand-hold on one of the green tentacles that were slowly crushing the life from his body. Thongor's hand slid along the surface of the topmost step of the dais—and closed about the glassy rondure of a slim ovoid.

*The demon exploded!*

One moment Thongor lay tightly enmeshed in a tangle of writhing emerald tendrils which were slowly tightening with steely strength—and the next instant the tendrils disintegrated into green vapor! The whirling vapor was flung from him by some tremendous power.

It was as if, out of nowhere, an invisible wall had sprung into being about the half-strangled warrior, and, thrusting in all directions outward from his body with unconquerable force, shattered the very substance of the tentacled demon—sundering it atom from atom with a burst of unthinkable power.

At the moment of the explosion, there came as well

a thunderous cry of indescribable torment, a bellowing howl of agony that shook the hall and sent the flames of the tall brass candelabra flickering.

Ald Turmis had but reached the base of the nine-tiered dais when this inexplicable event took place. The buffeting wind of the explosion knocked him to his knees. Openmouthed with astonishment, he stared about. Scudding wisps of green vapor were flying in every direction from the proximity of the barbarian, who lay prone and gasping for breath at the foot of the crystalline chair of thaumaturgy.

Even as he watched, Ald Turmis became aware that the demon was unable to re-form into a single wholeness again. For the shredded smoke was melting into emptiness even as it floated about the hall. Wisp after coiling wisp dissolved slowly. And, even as the last gobbling echoes of that demoniac bellow of unbearable agony faded in dying echoes, the last wisps of vapor disintegrated.

And the demon was—gone.

Atop the dais, Thongor stumbled to his feet, dragging in huge gulps of air into his starved lungs. He, too, peered about uncomprehendingly. Then, recalling the cold smooth cylinder his fumbling hand had chanced to grasp, he looked down at what he held in his hand. And he burst into croaking laughter.

"It seems I owe that foul toad of a priest, Kaman Thuu, a debt of thanks after all," he grunted hoarsely. And he held up his hand for Ald Turmis' inspection.

There in his palm lay—the Shield of Cathloda!

## 9. *The Return of the Sorcerer*

Thongor rejoined his comrade at the base of the dais. Despite the ferocity of the tentacled assault, and the steel strength of the constricting, snaky limbs, Thongor's massive body was unharmed. A few bruises, a few more aching muscles, a smear or two of blood where rasping, tightening ropes of sinewy tendril had torn away a few square inches of his tough hide—but nothing more serious than that.

"It was the talisman," he explained to Ald Turmis, "the protective amulet the old Zangabali priest lent me ere first I entered into this cursed and devil-haunted house! 'Tis proof against every ensorcellment—it nullifies every spell—drives thither every magical or demonic thing that comes near! Now that I think on it, the demon was helpless to harm me when I first encountered it. With devilish cunning, the hell-fiend assumed the form of a mortal wench, to beguile me. And once it had distracted my attention, it stole the talisman,—the Shield of Cathloda, as old Kaman Thuu called it—from my pocket-pouch."

"But—I don't understand!" Ald Turmis said, in a puzzled voice. "Why should—"

"If I had not borne the Shield on my person, the demon could have simply fallen on me the instant I entered the wizard's house and torn me apart—or tried to. But armed with the protection of the amulet, it was unable to do me hurt . . . at least, until it had seduced me with its girl-form and distracted my attention from the amulet!"

"I begin to see," the youth said slowly. "So it fetched the Shield of Cathloda here and set it beside our swords at the foot of the throne, in offering to its master when he should return from the sabbat."

"Aye," Thongor grunted. "And in my threshing about, I chanced to grasp the amulet, which automatically invoked its protective powers. The thing is small and glassy —I did not even notice it when I grabbed up our swords . . ."

"So when you seized upon the amulet, it tore the demon asunder. But why—how?"

Thongor shrugged impatiently. "How should I know? I know naught of sorcery and suchlike. Perchance it formed an invisible barrier about me, repelling the devil-thing. But it happened so swiftly, that the demon was blasted apart . . . and, since the amulet destroys the magical power of whatever ensorcelled thing it touches, the demon itself was demolished. For it must have been held present on the earth-plane by a powerful spell of black wizardry: 'tis abnormal for hell-spawn to gain entry into this plane of being; their natural home is far from here."

"So," mused Ald Turmis, "when the touch of the amulet canceled the spell which gave the demon freedom of movement on this plane, it disintegrated, returning to whatever crimson pit of hell was its natural place. And lucky for us it happened as it did, for the vile thing had well-nigh strangled the life out of you—and would have made short work of me, soon after!"

"Aye!" Thongor grunted, touching his bruised and swollen throat with tender fingers, grimacing with a wince of pain. "Thank Gorm I blundered on the crystal thing when I did. But, now, Ald Turmis, let us leave this accursed place, and swiftly. We have our swords, and here lie our cloaks and warrior harness. Let us shake the dust of this place off our heels, and repair to the nearest inn. 'Twill take a jug or two of strong red wine to wash the stink of magic from me, and I can taste it already!"

But Ald Turmis, looking past him to the top of the dais, made no answer. Instead he went pale to the lips and clutched Thongor's arm mutely.

Thongor grunted questioningly, and turned to see what had alarmed his comrade. And he saw—

Even as the ruddy glow of dawn lit the crystal dome above them and bathed the shadow-thronged hall with tremulous, bloody radiance, whirling darkness grew about the empty throne atop the tier of stone steps.

Was it the hell-spawned guardian, returning to this plane? Or was it—his master?

## 10. *The Living Statue*

Like a churning cloud of dust motes dancing in a skirl of wind, particles of darkness seethed about the sparkling crystal throne.

Gradually the whirling motes drew closer together, forming a shadowy pillar of darkness. Seven feet tall the blurred shadow-shape loomed. The vaporous fabric of its substance grew slowly solid.

The tall massive figure of a man melted out of the dense blackness. Tall and powerful he was, with a strong-boned swarthy face, wrapped from head to heel in a long black cloak whose collar lifted to peaks like horns beside his head.

"Gods of Hell!" Ald Turmis swore—*"The sorcerer returns!"*

And it was even so. Even as they watched, the heavy form became solid flesh. Still wrapped from throat to toe in the stiff black cloak, whose strange fabric glittered with tiny star-like points of light, the huge man stood. He seated himself in his chair of power and let long naked hands go out to clutch the arms of the chair. These

152

arms ended with great knobs carven from the sparkling crystal whereof the throne-chair was hewn, and each facet of these knobs bore inset a potent talisman of magic. Enthroned in his high place, touching with his naked hands the sigils which commanded unseen sources of power, the wizard was enshrined, invulnerable—a pole of power—the connecting node between the universe of matter and the unseen halfworld of tremendous forces which lay behind the structure of the cosmos.

Robed in power, beyond the reach of mortals, Athmar Phong gazed down at them calmly.

He was a veritable giant of a man. Had his towering height been less, he would have seemed a grossly fat man: as it was, his abnormal tallness made him seem less obese. But massive flesh lay on his giant bones. His weight must have been twice that of an ordinary man like Ald Turmis.

His face was a gross caricature of cold, cynical command. Hairless, massive-boned, he gazed down at them like some colossal buddha. His impassive, unlined face was a passionless mask of heavy flesh. Cold slitted eyes ringed in fat looked down at them with a placid contempt. There was callous cruelty in the set of his thick lips, brutal virility in the arrogant thrust of his hooked nose, remorseless and superhuman intelligence in the huge bulging brows of his naked pate.

"Thieves in my house," he said calmly, "and clever ones, at that. For, whether you know it or not, mortals, the guardian of my treasures was a demon of the seventh circle. I am amazed that mere men of brawn such as you had the cunning and the wit to destroy so mighty an entity of the transmundane."

His voice was like his face: heavy, slow, soft and cold. The words glided, oily and thick and sluggish, from almost motionless lips.

"Whomever sent you here, must have armed you with

153

a potent name of power. Let me warn you, then, think not to employ such a name against Athmar Phong. Enthroned, I sit at a nexus of the unseen forces, shielded from such powers as you might bear against me by currents of the ineffable. The name would rebound against yourself, leaving me unshaken. But let me see . . ."

The heavy, hooded eyelids lifted, baring orbs of utter blackness. No whites were visible about those blazing pupils: nor did they look like the eyes of a fully human creature.

Thongor stiffened, his senses stirring with an eerie chill of superstitious fear. The cold gaze of Athmar Phong thrust at him like needles of steel. His own gaze was locked and held in the grip of a superior will. He felt a weird sensation within his skull, as if cold tendrils of thought were prying through the secret places of his mind.

It lasted an instant only, and the tendrils were withdrawn.

Ominous satisfaction curved the lips of Athmar Phong in a slight, subtle smile.

"So it was my old friend, Kaman Thuu, sent you here, dog of a barbarian. I shall repay him trebly for this deed! Yonder youth also, as I recall, came thither at his urgings: him we took captive half-a-moon ago, and I thought him well secured in certain cellar chambers set aside for uninvited guests. I see the lad hath cunning enough to force an exit therefrom—or did you aid him with those great brawny arms, eh?"

Beside Thongor, Ald Turmis snarled an oath and his knuckles whitened on the hilt of his rapier. The Ptarthan wizard smiled cynically.

"I read your thoughts as well . . . rash, impetuous youth, 'tis best I immobilize the two of you before you cause hurt to yourself—"

Before either Thongor or Ald Turmis could think or

move or speak, the wizard's hand tightened on one of the talismans set within the hand-grip of his throne.

A spear of scintillating azure light speared from the crystal throne. The two young swordsmen stood bathed in the shaft of cold blue light, and the wizard smiled as Ald Turmis cried out sharply and Thongor growled an astonished oath.

"I—cannot—move!" the Zangabali cried in a voice of anguish.

His face gleamed wetly white, and as Thongor looked he saw an unnatural pallor sweep over the lean strong body of his comrade, who was naked but for a ragged clout.

"Numb . . . cold," Ald Turmis groaned. His voice sounded hoarse, constricted, as if the muscles of his throat were half-paralyzed. The wizard chuckled above them, a gloating sound that roused a warning growl in Thongor's deep chest. He, too, felt a momentary chill pass over his body as he stood in the path of the shaft of scintillant blue light. But then his fingers tightened over the cold ovoid shape of the Shield of Cathoda which he still clutched in his right hand, and the brief sensation of numbness vanished instantly.

The blue ray dimmed and died. The wizard withdrew his fingers from the circular sigil of blue metal.

"The immobilizing ray," he said softly. "Your flesh will slow grow harder and more dense until you twain will turn to stone. Lovely statues to adorn my hall . . . yet statues that live and think, for your souls will be held captive within your petrified flesh for all eternity to come. Fit punishment indeed, for the tools of that treacherous priestling, Kaman Thuu."

The giant wizard shifted in his throne. He stretched out one hand towards empty air.

"Poor mortals!" he said mockingly. "You searched my halls in vain, for that which you sought but could not find

155

was here beside my place all this while, though shielded from the gaze of uninvited guests. Behold—the mirror of Zaffar!"

One great naked hand clutched out at empty air and whisked aside a blur of bright cloth from a pedestal of glistening silver. Atop the silver stand an oval disc of thick black glass caught the dim radiance of dawn with sullen, shifting fires. Thongor stared.

The mirror had been covered with a strange cloth whose stiff fabric, bright, blurred, was oddly difficult to see. The eye would not quite focus on it; something about its blurred brilliance was eye-twisting, as if the sight slid off it. So the mirror had been beside the throne all the while!

Beside him, Ald Turmis moaned in anguish. His weird pallor was more visible now. The surface of his bare body, ashen white, looked rough and dry, almost . . . like stone.

And Thongor grimly knew that if he did not act, and soon, the young swordsman of Thurdis who had befriended him in the pits below this house of hell would turn to enduring stone—a living statue, imprisoning the tortured soul of Ald Turmis for all time to come!

## 11. *The Breaking of Spells*

The slow, heavy voice of Athmar Phong was speaking again, like the dull tolling of a leaden bell under thick water. Waves of words beat against them as the wizard droned on.

"Behold, O fortunate mortals, that which few eyes have ever looked upon—the supreme magical treasure of all the ages! Zaffar the Great, the mighty thaumaturge of Patanga wrought this mirror, and seven generations of time—as mortal men measure time—went into the making thereof! Seven thousand potent spells of power are sealed into the substance of this black mirror. Zaffar fashioned it from perdurable adamant, the strongest substance known to sorcery. Now it is fragile as glass . . . and bound helpless and raging therein, lieth forever imprisoned the very self and substance of Aqquoonkagua, one of the nine thousand princes of the infernal pit! Aye, a mighty and eternal prince of hell, older than the very universe of stars itself—a fragment of elder chaos and old night—caught and held with within the magic mirror of Zaffar the Great! *Behold*—"

The black mirror was about the size ·of the *cherm*, the small, lightweight buckler the Lemurian warriors wore strapped to their left forearms. It was black as the heart of darkness itself, a disk of shimmering crystal thick as the breath of two fingers.

As Athmar Phong touched it with his naked hands, it stirred with strange life. Thongor felt his hackles rise upon the back of his neck. *Within the shimmering darkness, a crimson shadow—moved!*

For a moment Thongor glimpsed a great triangular head. As he watched, it shouldered into view, peering through the mirror as through a black window. He saw one great glaring eye—a pit of blazing hellfire—and a wide, fanged maw open, working, screaming with silent fury. Then the red thing that was a captive Prince of the Pit slunk back into the darkness of its shadowy home and was lost to view.

"Gorm!" the Barbarian grunted, feeling sweat trickle down his sides and bedew his brows. Strange and terrible were the ways of wizards; dark and dreadful were their uncanny arts. The mighty crimson demon was somehow reduced to two dimensions only: to him the flat surface of the mirror was an entire world, from which he could never break free unless released by an outside agency.

157

The whole thing was mad and nightmarish. For an instant he almost pitied the shambling scarlet horror locked in the surface of the ebon glass for dim, unguessable aeons . . .

A groan of mute suffering from the young swordsman at his side awoke Thongor from these dark thoughts. Ald Turmis, too, was imprisoned—and his prison was his own living flesh, slowly, inch by inch, petrifying into solid stone. A doom darker and more terrible even than that of the enslaved Demon Prince . . .

It was time for Thongor to act.

He had not moved since the Ptarthan wizard had sent the strange beam of azure radiance sweeping over him and his companion.

Secure in his high place, throned in the midst of his magical forces at the nexus of two universes, Athmar Phong little dreamed that the young barbarian was not rendered helpless from the eerie power of the immobilizing ray. But now Thongor swung into action.

He reached out and laid his hand upon the shoulder of Ald Turmis—the hand that held the all-potent Shield of Cathloda. The flesh of his comrade was harsh, dry, rough and cold to his touch. The surface of the young Zangabali's skin felt strangely granular. But the nullifying powers of the protective amulet were enormous—strong enough to whelm the spell of the blue ray, aye, and far stronger, as would soon be seen!

Ald Turmis cried out as the amulet touched his hardening flesh. A tingle of weird force swept through his body, like the shuddering electric force of lightning. Through every cell and organ, every gland and muscle and tissue of his body it swept, and the spell of Athmar Phong ebbed and died before it. The young swordsman, suddenly freed from the effects of the spell, staggered and fell to one knee, gasping with relief.

On the sparkling crystal throne, Athmar Phong froze

158

with utter astonishment. Thongor tossed back his unshorn mane and roared with laughter.

"Now, wizard—if swords cannot battle against sorcery, we will see what happens when I pit magic against—magic!" he thundered.

And before the wizard could move or think, Thongor whipped back his mighty arm—and hurled the all-potent amulet straight at the black mirror of Zaffar!

It flew glittering through the dawnlit air. Straight as an arrow to its mark it sped, and when it touched the invisible forces that wove a viewless shield about the wizard's throne of power, great spells were broken. Canceled energies flashed through the spectrum of visible light. A terrific flash of eye-searing radiance lit the hall like some supernal sun.

Tears pouring from his blinded eyes, Athmar Phong screamed terribly, high and shrill like an animal in pain. He lurched unsteadily to his feet, pawing at his seared eyes.

Hurled with the irresistible strength of Thongor's mighy arm, the Shield of Cathloda flew through the flashing energy field—and crashed full into the black mirror.

The mirror came apart in a dark flash of released forces—it shattered to grains of black dust!

For a single flashing instant, as age-old spells were broken, tremendous energy was released. A seething ball of black flame surged about the crystal throne. The silver pedestal, at the very node and nexus of the canceled binding forces, flashed with intolerable heat. It glowed crimson, then canary, then blinding white. It slumped, crumbling slowly, like the shaft of a waxen candle suddenly thrust into the roaring heart of a furnace. Glowing rivulets of molten metal slithered sluggishly over the topmost tier of the dais like serpents of liquid flame.

One blazing rivulet crawled between the staggering

159

legs of the blinded, howling wizard. His glistening black cloak went up in a puff of fire. Suddenly sheathed from throat to heel in a sheet of crackling flame, the wizard screeched and fell flopping and writhing to the steps. He rolled down them and crashed against the stone pave of the hall, crushing out the flames beneath his heavy weight. Panting, his flesh blistered and blackened, he staggered to his knees, sobbing with agony and naked fury.

But neither Thongor nor Ald Turmis could spare a glance for the unthroned sorceror. Their gaze was riveted with horrible fascination at that which stood above the dais.

For the Shield of Cathloda had severed the seven thousand spells which had bound the Demon Prince within the depths of the enchanted glass.

*Now Aqquoonkagua was free!*

## 12. *Flames of Hell*

Up out of the whirling cloud of black flame towered and grew a titanic shape of terror.

Crimson it was, and covered with crawling fire; bestial of shape, hulking and monstrous. It had great sloping shoulders like some mighty ape, from which long arms swung, arms that ended in great three-clawed paws, that also smoldered and smoked as if molded out of red-hot iron.

Up and up it went until it loomed forty feet about the stone pavement. Flames slithered across its shaggy skin; the fiery red light that beat up from it was dazzling. The room swirled with smoke. Blistering heat like the breath of an open furnace went baking across the hall in waves. Soot blackened the walls and hung thick in the air.

Roaring, raging, the crimson thing stood free after long weary centuries of time.

It had no neck. A heavy-jawed, apelike head swung between the burly crimson shoulders. One huge eye blazed with fires of madness under beetling brows. The fanged maw gaped and slavered.

One great paw closed into a fist and came smashing down on the sot-blackened, overturned throne. It burst to fragments, and was ground to dust under the weight of the blow. The other paw reached down for Athmar Phong.

Naked, the wizard's heavy body sprawled panting at the foot of the dais. Blind and horribly burnt, the Ptarthan sorceror somehow knew or guessed what was about to happen. Like a huge fat slug writhing under the gardener's hoe, he squalled and wriggled on the hot pave as the titanic flaming hand came down upon him. Waves of heat beat from the grasping paw, crisping flesh and withering cloth to ash. The demon's hand was huge as the wizard's body, and the three mighty claws were big as smouldering logs. The searing heat of the demon's flesh smote him first, and he kicked and screamed. Then the hand came down upon him and snatched him up.

Thongor had seen much of battle and death and suffering, but never had he heard such a cry wrung from mortal lips as that which now went ringing through the hall. A hoarse, terrible, bellow of ultimate agony and unutterable despair—the sort of cry that rips the lining of the human throat.

The naked wizard flopped and wriggled on the flaming palm of the demon's hand. Then the burning claws closed over him slowly—tightened—and the screams were cut off. The sickening stench of broiling human flesh filled the great hall. Ald Turmis gagged and spat; Thongor's own gorge rose at the nauseating smell.

Bearing the smoking corpse of Athmar Phong in one

great paw the roaring, raging demon burst up through the dome of dawnlit crystal and was gone—back to whatever ultracosmic hell the blasphemous rituals of the thaumaturge Zaffar had conjured it from, ages ago.

The broken dome collapsed, strewing the soot-smeared pave with shattered wreckage. Mighty stone pillars, shoved askew by the demon's skyward passage, toppled slowly, shaking the wizard's house to its foundations as they came crashing down. Black cracks zigzagged through the fabric of the walls. The house was coming down upon their heads.

Thongor grabbed Ald Turmis by the shoulder, shouting through the roar of wreckage. They ran across the buckling stone flags for the yawning blackness of the secret panel which still stood open. Thongor snatched up their cloaks and harnesses as they sprinted for freedom.

The terrific heat of the demon's crimson body had touched to flame the tapestries and hangings in the hall. Overturned benches and fallen beams blazed like oil-soaked torches. The ruined hall was transformed into a thundering inferno within mere instants.

The two warriors plunged into the black door and vanished from view. Down the secret passageways they went. Room after room, as they passed, was bursting into flame. It was weird to see solid marble burn, and metal, and crystal, too. The fires that blazed within the demon's body were the fires of some ultracosmic inferno—hotter than any flames of man's knowledge. The terrible hellfire burned through stone walls and floors, consuming everything in its path like a ravenous dragon.

And thus it was that doom came down upon the house of Athmar Phong and he was nevermore seen by the eyes of men.

## 13. *A New Day Dawns*

The morning breeze blew fresh and clean from the great Gulf of Patanga, and the tang of the wet salt sea was upon it. They drew deep lungfuls of cold fresh air with hearty zest after the stench of the burning house and the reeking slime of the subterranean passage.

It was good to be alive, and free, watching the sun come up over the shoulder of the world. All things looked pure and clean and new in the clear strong light, and the horrors of the night were over and done. Thongor drank deep of cold red wine and stretched out his weary legs with a grunt of satisfaction.

They had found the secret door in the pits, the door that led to the branching ways of the subterranean network of tunnels beneath the city, and for a time they had followed the yellow Yan Hu characters that marked the way back to the Temple of Seven Gods. But Thongor had not survived this long in the Land of Peril—as the *Scarlet Edda* named all these realms of the devil-haunted southlands—without evolving a strong and canny sense of survival. Why return empty-handed to the gaunt, scheming priest? He would pay nothing for a task undone—and Kaman Thuu would not be very happy to learn the black mirror was now destroyed for all time. Instead, the barbarian recalled what the priest had said about Shan Yom glyphs wherewith side tunnels were blazoned in scarlet glowing pigment. Hence he and Ald Turmis had taken this route, and come out in an empty alleyway beside the seafront where tall ships rode at anchor, waiting on the morning tide.

The two youths were filthy, hungry and exhausted from the trials of their night in the house of hell. But it would have been unlike Thongor to have come forth empy-handed from the wizard's house; so he had lingered for a moment in one of the lower chambers to snatch up a gemmed ornament or two wherewith he and Ald Turmis had purchased themselves a hearty breakfast in the quayside tavern called The Sailor's Haven.

Across the rooftops of the city, a pillar of oily black smoke stood against the pure morning skies. Blue and scarlet flames flickered through it strangely. The house of Athmar Phong was burnt to ashes and all his terrible sorceries were dust, aye, and the loathsome mewling hybirds of his blasphemous experiments in life-making had gone to rest at last and were freed forever from the torment of living. But still the rubble burned.

"Whither now?" Thongor grunted to his companion. Ald Turmis emptied the last drop of wine from their third bottle and sat back with a sigh of repletion.

"The gods know, friend," he said. "But one thing at least is certain: 'twould be unhealthy for the two of us to remain here in Zangabal for long. Kaman Thuu has long arms and many cunning fingers. And he will not like this night's black business, you may set a wager on that!"

"I know," Thongor grunted lazily. "I have a mind to see the gates of Zangabal close shut behind my back, and to strike out for another city. What about this Thurdis, the Dragon City across the Gulf, whereof you spoke earlier?"

"Well, why not?" said Ald Turmis. "Phal Thurid, Sark of Thurdis, arms himself for conquest and I have heard he enlists a mighty host of warriors. Surely there is a place among his warriors for your mighty broadsword, and my rapier. Shall we try our fortunes in the ranks of the mercenaries? There is a merchant galley flies the Dragon of Thurdis at the ninth quay. They sail with the early morning tide, and if you have any gold left after purchasing this magnificent feast whereof I can eat not a single bite more, perchance we can buy passage thither to Thurdis. Shall we go together for a while, Thongor, and see what Fate has in store for us?"

Thongor stretched lazily, like a great cat. His black cloak was slung about his bare bronze shoulders, and a gold coin or two still nested in the pocket-pouch of his warrior's harness. He ached to shake the dust of Zangabal from his heels, and to feel the gulf-wind blow fresh and clean in his face, and to explore the winding ways of a new city for a time.

"Well, why not?" he growled, and thus it was decided.

And thus were the feet of Thongor set upon the path that would lead him into the fullness of time to a destiny stranger and more glorious than that of other men.

But that is another story. . . .

*Conan the Cimmerian, elemental and seemingly indestructible, looms larger than life when contrasted with the hero figures of our times. Here is an adventure from the days when he was already known and justly feared by those who, evoking dark and ancient forces, worshiped at the shrines of the evil ones.*

# A WITCH SHALL BE BORN

## by Robert E. Howard

# A WITCH SHALL BE BORN

## 1. *The Blood-Red Crescent*

TARAMIS, Queen of Khauran, awakened from a dream-haunted slumber to a silence that seemed more like the stillness of nighted catacombs than the normal quiet of a sleeping palace. She lay staring into the darkness, wondering why the candles in their golden candelabra had gone out. A flecking of stars marked a gold-barred casement that lent no illumination to the interior of the chamber. But, as Taramis lay there, she became aware of a spot of radiance glowing in the darkness before her. She watched, puzzled. It grew, and its intensity deepened as it expanded, a widening disk of lurid light hovering against the dark velvet hangings of the opposite wall. Taramis caught her breath, starting up to a sitting position. A dark object was visible in that circle of light—*a human head.*

In a sudden panic the queen opened her lips to cry out for her maids; then she checked herself. The glow was more lurid, the head more vividly limned. It was a woman's head, small, delicately molded, superbly poised, with a high-piled mass of lustrous black hair. The face grew distinct as she stared—and it was the sight of this face which froze the cry in Taramis' throat. The features were her own! She might have been looking into a mirror which subtly altered her reflection, lending it a tigerish gleam of eye, a vindictive curl of lip.

"Ishtar!" gasped Taramis. "I am bewitched!"

Appallingly, the apparition spoke, and its voice was like honeyed venom.

"Bewitched? No, sweet sister! Here is no sorcery."

169

"Sister?" stammered the bewildered girl. "I have no sister."

"You never had a sister?" came the sweet, poisonously mocking voice. "Never a twin sister whose flesh was as soft as yours to caress or hurt?"

"Why, once I had a sister," answered Taramis, still convinced that she was in the grip of some sort of nightmare. "But she died."

The beautiful face in the disk was convulsed with the aspect of a fury; so hellish became its expression that Taramis, cowering back, half expected to see snaky locks writhe hissing about the ivory brow.

"You lie!" The accusation was spat from between the snarling red lips. "She did not die! Fool! Oh, enough of this mummery! Look—and let your sight be blasted!"

Light ran suddenly along the hangings like flaming serpents, and incredibly the candles in the golden sticks flared up again. Taramis crouched on her velvet couch, her lithe legs flexed beneath her, staring wide-eyed at the pantherish figure which posed mockingly before her. It was as if she gazed upon another Taramis, identical with herself in every contour of feature and limb, yet animated by an alien and evil personality. The face of this stranger waif reflected the opposite of every characteristic the countenance of the queen denoted. Lust and mystery sparkled in her scintillant eyes, cruelty lurked in the curl of her full red lips. Each movement of her supple body was subtly suggestive. Her coiffure imitated that of the queen's, on her feet were gilded sandals such as Taramis wore in her boudoir. The sleeveless, low-necked silk tunic, girdled at the waist with a cloth-of-gold cincture, was a duplicate of the queen's night-garment.

"Who are you?" gasped Taramis, an icy chill she could not explain creeping along her spine. "Explain

170

your presence before I call my ladies-in-waiting to summon the guard!"

"Scream until the roof beams crack," callously answered the stranger. "Your sluts will not wake till dawn, though the palace spring into flames about them. Your guardsmen will not hear your squeals; they have been sent out of this wing of the palace."

"What!" exclaimed Taramis, stiffening with outraged majesty. "Who dared give my guardsmen such a command?"

"I did, sweet sister," sneered the other girl. "A little while ago, before I entered. They thought it was their darling adored queen. Ha! How beautifully I acted the part! With what imperious dignity, sofened by womanly sweetness, did I address the great louts who knelt in their armor and plumed helmets!"

Taramis felt as if a stifling net of bewilderment was being drawn about her.

"Who are you?" she cried desperately. "What madness is this? Why do you come here?"

"Who am I?" There was the spite of a she-cobra's hiss in the soft response. The girl stepped to the edge of the couch, grasped the queen's white shoulders with fierce fingers, and bent to glare full into the startled eyes of Taramis. And under the spell of that hypnotic glare, the queen forgot to resent the unprecedented outrage of violent hands laid on regal flesh.

"Fool!" gritted the girl between her teeth. "Can you ask? Can you wonder? I am Salome!"

"Salome!" Taramis breathed the word, and the hairs prickled on her scalp as she realized the incredible, numbing truth of the statement. "I thought you died within the hour of your birth," she said feebly.

"So thought many," answered the woman who called herself Salome. "They carried me into the desert to die, damn them! I, a mewing, puling babe whose life was so

171

young it was scarcely the flicker of a candle. And do you know why they bore me forth to die?"

"I—I have heard the story——" faltered Taramis.

Salome laughed fiercely, and slapped her bosom. The low-necked tunic left the upper parts of her firm breasts bare, and between them there shone a curious mark—a crescent, red as blood.

"The mark of the witch!" cried Taramis, recoiling.

"Aye!" Salome's laughter was dagger-edged with hate. "The curse of the kings of Khauran! Aye, they tell the tale in the market places, with wagging beards and rolling eyes, the pious fools! They tell how the first queen of our line had traffic with a fiend of darkness and bore him a daughter who lives in foul legendry to this day. And thereafter, in each century, a girl baby was born into the Askhaurian dynasty, with a scarlet half-moon between her breasts, that signified her destiny.

" 'Every century a witch shall be born.' So ran the ancient curse. And so it has come to pass. Some were slain at birth, as they sought to slay me. Some walked the earth as witches, proud daughters of Khauran, with the moon of hell burning upon their ivory bosoms. Each was named Salome. I, too, am Salome. It was always Salome, the witch. It will always be Salome, the witch, even when the mountains of ice have roared down from the pole and ground the civilizations to ruin, and a new world has risen from the ashes and dust—even then there shall be Salomes to walk the earth, to trap men's hearts by their sorcery, to dance before the kings of the world, and see the heads of the wise men fall at their pleasure."

"But—but you——" stammered Taramis.

"I?" The scintillant eyes burned like dark fires of mystery. "They carried me into the desert far from the city, and laid me naked on the hot sand, under the flaming sun. And then they rode away and left me for the jackals and the vultures and the desert wolves.

"But the life in me was stronger than the life in common folk, for it partakes of the essence of the forces that seethe in the black gulfs beyond mortal ken. The hours passed, and the sun slashed down like the molten flames of Hell, but I did not die—aye, something of that torment I remember, faintly and far away, as one remembers a dim, formless dream. Then there were camels, and yellow-skinned men who wore silk robes and spoke in a weird tongue. Strayed from the caravan road, they passed close by, and their leader saw me, and recognized the scarlet crescent on my bosom. He took me up and gave me life.

"He was a magician from far Khitai, returning to his native kingdom after a journey to Stygia. He took me with him to purple-towered Paikang, its minarets rising amid the vine-festooned jungles of bamboo, and there I grew to womanhood under his teaching. Age had steeped him deep in black wisdom, not weakened his powers of evil. Many things he taught me——"

She paused, smiling enigmatically, with wicked mystery gleaming in her dark eyes. Then she tossed her head.

"He drove me from him at last, saying that I was but a common witch in spite of his teachings, and not fit to command the mighty sorcery he would have taught me. He would have made me queen of the world and ruled the nations through me, he said, but I was only a harlot of darkness. But what of it? I could never endure to seclude myself in a golden tower, and spend the long hours staring into a crystal globe, mumbling over incantations written on serpent's skin in the blood of virgins, poring over musty volumes in forgotten languages.

"He said I was but an earthly sprite, knowing naught of the deeper gulfs of cosmic sorcery. Well, this world contains all I desire—power, and pomp, and glittering pageantry, handsome men and soft women for my paramours and my slaves. He had told me who I was, of the

173

curse and my heritage. I have returned to take that to which I have as much right as you. Now it is mine by right of possession."

"What do you mean?" Taramis sprang up and faced her sister, strung out of her bewilderment and fright. "Do you imagine that by drugging a few of my maids and tricking a few of my guardsmen you have established a claim to the throne of Khauran? Do not forget that I am queen of Khauran! I shall give you a place of honor, as my sister, but——"

Salome laughed hatefully.

"How generous of you, dear, sweet sister! But before you begin putting me in my place—perhaps you will tell me whose soldiers camp in the plain outside the city walls?"

"They are the Shemitish mercenaries of Constantius, the Kothic *voivode* of the Free Companies."

"And what do they in Khauran?" cooed Salome.

Taramis felt that she was being subtly mocked, but she answered with an assumption of dignity which she scarcely felt.

"Constantius staked permission to pass along the borders of Khauran on his way to Turan. He himself is hostage for their good behavior as long as they are within my domains."

"And Constantius," pursued Salome. "Did he not ask your hand today?"

Taramis shot her a clouded glance of suspicion.

"How did you know that?"

An insolent shrug of the slim, naked shoulders was the only reply.

"You refused, dear sister?"

"Certainly I refused!" exclaimed Taramis angrily. "Do you, an Askhaurian princess yourself, suppose that the queen of Khauran could treat such a proposal with anything but disdain? Wed a bloody-handed adventurer, a

174

man exiled from his own kingdom because of his crimes, and the leader of organized plunderers and hired murderers?

"I should never have allowed him to bring his black-bearded slayers into Khauran. But he is virtually a prisoner in the south tower, guarded by my soldiers. Tomorrow I shall bid him order his troops to leave the kingdom. He himself shall be kept captive until they are over the border. Meantime, my soldiers man the walls of the city, and I have warned him that he will answer for any outrages perpetrated on the villagers or shepherds by his mercenaries."

"He is confined in the south tower?" asked Salome.

"That is what I said. Why do you ask?"

For answer Salome clapped her hands, and lifting her voice, with a gurgle of cruel mirth in it, called: "The queen grants you an audience, Falcon!"

A gold-arabesqued door opened and a tall figure entered the chamber, at the sight of which Taramis cried out in amazement and anger.

"Constantius! You dare enter my chamber!"

"As you see, Your Majesty!" He bent his dark, hawk-like head in mock humility.

Constantius, whom men called Falcon, was tall, broad-shouldered, slim-waisted, lithe and strong as pliant steel. He was handsome in an aquiline, ruthless way. His face was burnt dark by the sun, and his hair, which grew far back fron his high, narrow forehead, was black as a raven. His dark eyes were penetrating and alert, the hardness of his thin lips not softened by his thin black mustache. His boots were of Kordavan leather, his hose and doublet of plain, dark silk, tarnished with the wear of the camps and the stains of armor rust.

Twisting his mustache, he let his gaze travel up and down the shrinking queen with an effrontery that made her wince.

"By Ishtar, Taramis," he said silkily, "I find you more alluring in your night-tunic than in your queenly robes. Truly, this is an auspicious night!"

Fear grew in the queen's dark eyes. She was no fool; she knew that Constantius would never dare this outrage unless he was sure of himself.

"You are mad!" she said. "If I am in your power in this chamber, you are no less in the power of my subjects, who will rend you to pieces if you touch me. Go at once, if you would live."

Both laughed mockingly, and Salome made an impatient gesture.

"Enough of this farce; let us on to the next act in the comedy. Listen, dear sister: it was I who sent Constantius here. When I decided to take the throne of Khauran, I cast about for a man to aid me, and chose the Falcon, because of his utter lack of all characteristics men call good."

"I am overwhelmed, princess," murmured Constantius sardonically, with a profound bow.

"I sent him to Khauran and, once his men were camped in the plain outside and he was in the palace, I entered the city by that small gate in the west wall—the fools guarding it thought it was you returning from some nocturnal adventure——"

"You hell-cat!" Taramis' cheeks flamed and her resentment got the better of her regal reserve.

Salome smiled hardly.

"They were properly surprised and shocked, but admitted me without question. I entered the palace the same way and gave the order to the surprised guards that sent them marching away, as well as the men who guarded Constantius in the south tower. Then I came here, attending to the ladies-in-waiting on the way."

Taramis' fingers clenched and she paled.

"Well, what next?" she asked in a shaky voice.

"Listen!" Salome inclined her head. Faintly through the casement there came the clank of marching men in armor; gruff voices shouted in an alien tongue, and cries of alarm mingled with the shouts.

"The people awaken and grow fearful," said Constantius sardonically. "You had better go and reassure them, Salome!"

"Call me Taramis," answered Salome. "We must become accustomed to it."

"What have you done?" cried Taramis. "What have you done?"

"I have gone to the gates and ordered the soldiers to open them," answered Salome. "They were astounded, but they obeyed. This is the Falcon's army you hear, marching into the city."

"You devil!" cried Taramis. "You have betrayed my people, in my guise! You have made me seem a traitor! Oh, I shall go to them——"

With a cruel laugh Salome caught her wrist and jerked her back. The magnificent suppleness of the queen was helpless against the vindictive strength that steeled Salome's slender limbs.

"You know how to reach the dungeons from the palace, Constantius?" said the witch-girl. "Good. Take this spitfire and lock her into the strongest cell. The jailers are all sound in drugged sleep. I saw to that. Send a man to cut their throats before they can awaken. None must ever know what has occurred tonight. Henceforward I am Taramis, and Taramis is a nameless prisoner in an unknown dungeon."

Constantius smiled with a glint of strong white teeth under his thin mustache.

"Very good; but you would not deny me a little—ah—amusement first?"

"Not I! Tame the scornful hussy as you will." With a wicked laugh Salome flung her sister into the Kothian's arms, and turned away through the door that opened into the outer corridor.

Fright widened Taramis' lovely eyes, her supple figure rigid and straining against Constantius' embrace. She forgot the men marching in the streets, forgot the outrage to her queenship, in the face of the menace to her womanhood. She forgot all sensations but terror and shame as she faced the complete cynicism of Constantius' burning, mocking eyes, felt his hard arms crushing her writhing body.

Salome, hurrying along the corridor outside, smiled spitefully as a scream of despair and agony rang shuddering through the palace.

## 2. *The Tree of Death*

The young soldier's hose and shirt were smeared with dried blood, wet with sweat and gray with dust. Blood oozed from the deep gash in his thigh, from the cuts on his breast and shoulder. Perspiration glistened on his livid face and his fingers were knotted in the cover of the divan on which he lay. Yet his words reflected mental suffering that outweighed physical pain.

"She must be mad!" he repeated again and again, like one still stunned by some monstrous and incredible happening. "It's like a nightmare! Taramis, whom all Khauran loves, betraying her people to that devil from Koth! Oh, Ishtar, why was I not slain? Better die than live to see our queen turn traitor and harlot!"

"Lie still, Valerius," begged the girl who was washing and bandaging his wounds with trembling hands. "Oh, please lie still, darling! You will make your wounds worse. I dared not summon a leech——"

"No," muttered the wounded youth. "Constantius'

blue-bearded devils will be searching the quarters for wounded Khauranis; they'll hang every man who has wounds to show he fought against them. Oh, Taramis, how could you betray the people who worshipped you?" In his fierce agony he writhed, weeping in rage and shame, and the terrified girl caught him in her arms, straining his tossing head against her bosom, imploring him to be quiet.

"Better death than the black shame that has come upon Khauran this day," he groaned. "Did you see it, Ivga?"

"No, Valerius." Her soft, nimble fingers were again at work, gently cleansing and closing the gaping edges of his raw wounds. "I was awakened by the noise of fighting in the streets—I looked out a casement and saw the Shemites cutting down people; then presently I heard you calling me faintly from the alley door."

"I had reached the limits of my strength," he muttered. "I fell in the alley and could not rise. I knew they'd find me soon if I lay there—I killed three of the blue-bearded beasts, by Ishtar! They'll never swagger through Khauran's streets, by the gods! The fiends are tearing their hearts in Hell!"

The trembling girl crooned soothingly to him, as to a wounded child, and closed his panting lips with her own cool sweet mouth. But the fire that raged in his soul would not allow him to lie silent.

"I was not on the wall when the Shemites entered," he burst out. "I was asleep in the barracks, with the others not on duty. It was just before dawn when our captain entered, and his face was pale under his helmet. 'The Shemites are in the city,' he said. 'The queen came to the southern gate and gave orders that they should be admitted. She made the men come down from the walls, where they've been on guard since Constantius entered the kingdom. I don't understand it, and neither does anyone else, but I heard her give the order, and we obeyed as we always do. We are ordered to assemble in the square before the palace. Form ranks outside the barracks and march—leave your arms and armor here. Ishtar knows what this means, but it is the queen's order."

"Well, when we came to the square the Shemites were drawn up on foot opposite the palace, ten thousand of the blue-bearded devils, fully armed, and people's heads were thrust out of every window and door on the square. The streets leading into the square were thronged by bewildered folk. Taramis was standing on the steps of the palace, alone except for Constantius, who stood stroking his mustache like a great lean cat who has just devoured a sparrow. But fifty Shemites with bows in their hands were ranged below them.

"That's where the queen's guard should have been, but they were drawn up at the foot of the palace stair, as puzzled as we, though they had come fully armed, in spite of the queen's order.

"Taramis spoke to us then, and told us that she had reconsidered the proposal made her by Constantius—why, only yesterday she threw it in his teeth in open court!—and that she had decided to make him her royal consort. She did not explain why she had brought the Shemites into the city so treacherously. But she said that, as Constantius had control of a body of professional fighting-men, the army of Khauran would no longer be needed, and therefore she disbanded it, and ordered us to go quietly to our homes.

"Why, obedience to our queen is second nature to us, but we were struck dumb and found no word to answer. We broke ranks almost before we knew what we were doing, like men in a daze.

"But, when the palace guard was ordered to disarm likewise and disband, the captain of the guard, Conan, interrupted. Men said he was off duty the night before, and drunk. But he was wide awake now. He shouted to the guardsmen to stand as they were until they received an order from him—and such is his dominance of his men, that they obeyed in spite of the queen. He strode up to the palace steps and glared at Taramis—and then he roared: "This is not the queen! This isn't Taramis! It's some devil in masquerade!"

"Then Hell was to pay! I don't know just what happened. I think a Shemite struck Conan, and Conan killed him. The next instant the square was a battleground. The Shemites fell on the guardsmen, and their spears and arrows struck down many soldiers who had already disbanded.

"Some of us grabbed up such weapons as we could and fought back. We hardly knew what we were fighting for, but it was against Constantius and his devils—not against Taramis, I swear it! Constantius shouted to cut the traitors down. We were not traitors!" Despair and bewilderment shook his voice. The girl murmured pityingly, not understanding it all, but aching in sympathy with her lover's suffering.

"The people did not know which side to take. It was a madhouse of confusion and bewilderment. We who fought didn't have a chance, in no formation, without armor and only half armed. The guards were fully armed and drawn up in a square, but there were only five hundred of them. They took a heavy toll before they were cut down, but there could be only one conclusion to such a battle. And while her people were being slaughtered before her, Taramis stood on the palace steps, with Constantius' arm about her waist, and laughed like a heartless, beautiful fiend! Gods, it's all mad—mad!

"I never saw a man fight as Conan fought. He put his back to the courtyard wall, and before they overpowered him the dead men were strewn in heaps thigh-deep about him. But at last they dragged him down, a hundred against one. When I saw him fall I dragged myself away, feeling as if the world had burst under my very fingers. I heard Constantius call to his dogs to take the captain alive—stroking his mustache, with that hateful smile on his lips!"

That smile was on the lips of Constantius at that very moment. He sat his horse among a cluster of his men—thick-bodied Shemites with curled blue-black beards and hooked noses; the low-swinging sun struck glints from their peaked helmets and the silvered scales of their corselets. Nearly a mile behind, the walls and towers of Khauran rose sheer out of the meadowlands.

By the side of the caravan road a heavy cross had been planted, and on this grim tree a man hung, nailed there by iron spikes through his hands and feet. Naked but for a loincloth, the man was almost a giant in stature, and his muscles stood out in thick corded ridges on limbs and body, which the sun had long ago burned brown. The perspiration of agony beaded his face and his mighty breast, but from under the tangled black mane that fell over his low, broad forehead, his blue eyes blazed with an unquenched fire. Blood oozed sluggishly from the lacerations in his hands and feet.

Constantius saluted him mockingly.

"I am sorry, captain," he said, "that I can not remain to ease your last hours, but I have duties to perform in yonder city—I must not keep our delicious queen waiting!" He laughed softly. "So I leave you to your own devices—and those beauties!" He pointed meaningly at the black shadows which swept incessantly back and forth, high above.

"Were it not for them, I imagine that a powerful brute like yourself should live on the cross for days. Do not cherish any illusions of rescue because I am leaving you unguarded. I have had it proclaimed that anyone seeking to take your body, living or dead, from the cross, will be flayed alive, together with all the members of his family, in the public square. I am so firmly established in Khauran that my order is as good as a regiment of guardsmen. I am leaving no guard, because the vultures will not approach as long as anyone is near, and I do not wish them to feel any constraint. That is also why I brought you so far from the city. These desert vultures approach the walls no closer than this spot.

"And so, brave captain, farewell! I will remember you when, in an hour, Taramis lies in my arms."

Blood started afresh from the pierced palms as the victim's mallet-like fists clenched convulsively on the spike-heads. Knots and bunches of muscle started out on the massive arms, and Conan bent his head forward and spat savagely at Constantius' face. The *voivode* laughed coolly, wiped the saliva from his gorget and reined his horse about.

"Remember me when the vultures are tearing at your living flesh," he called mockingly. "The desert scavengers are a particularly voracious breed. I have seen men hang for hours on a cross, eyeless, earless, and scalpless, before the sharp beaks had eaten their way into his vitals."

Without a backward glance he rode toward the city, a supple, erect figure, gleaming in his burnished armor, his stolid, bearded henchmen jogging beside him. A faint rising of dust from the worn trail marked their passing.

The man hanging on the cross was the one touch of sentient life in a landscape that seemed desolate and deserted in the late evening. Khauran, less than a mile away, might have been on the other side of the world, and existing in another age.

Shaking the sweat out of his eyes, Conan stared blankly at the familiar terrain. On either side of the city, and beyond it, stretched the fertile meadowlands, with cattle browsing in the distance where fields and vineyards checkered the plain. The western and northern horizons were dotted with villages, miniature in the distance. A lesser distance to the southeast, a silvery gleam marked the course of a river, and beyond that river sandy desert began abruptly, to stretch away and away beyond the horizon. Conan stared at that expanse of empty waste, shimmering tawnily in the late sunlight, as a trapped hawk stares at the open sky. A revulsion shook him when he glanced at the gleaming towers of Khauran. The city had betrayed him—trapped him into circumstances that left him hanging to a wooden cross like a hare nailed to a tree.

A red lust for vengeance swept away the thought. Curses ebbed fitfully from the man's lips. All his universe contracted, focused, became incorporated in the four iron spikes that held him from life and freedom. His great muscles quivered, knotting like iron cables. With the sweat starting out on his graying skin, he sought to gain leverage, to tear the nails from the wood. It was useless. They had been driven deep. Then he tried to tear his hands off the spikes, and it was not the knifing abysmal agony that finally caused him to cease his efforts, but the futility of it. The spike heads were broad and heavy; he could not drag them through the wounds. A surge of helplessness shook the giant for the first time in his life. He hung motionless, his head resting on his breast, shutting his eyes against the aching glare of the sun.

A beat of wings caused him to look up, just as a feathered shadow shot down out of the sky. A keen beak, stabbing at his eyes, cut his cheek, and he jerked his head aside, shutting his eyes involuntarily. He shouted, a croaking, desperate shout of menace, and the vultures swerved away and retreated, frightened by the sound. They resumed their way circling above his head. Blood trickled over Conan's mouth; he licked his lips involuntarily, spat at the salty taste.

Thirst assailed him savagely. He had drunk deeply of wine the night before, and no water had touched his lips since before the battle in the square, that dawn. And killing was thirsty, salt-sweaty work. He gared at the distant river as a man in Hell glares through the opened grille. He thought of gushing freshets of white water he had breasted, laved to the shoulders in liquid jade. He remembered great horns of foaming ale; jacks of sparkling wine gulped carelessly or spilled on the tavern floor. He bit his lip to keep from bellowing in intolerable anguish as a tortured animal bellows.

The sun sank, a lurid ball in a fiery sea of blood. Against a crimson rampart that banded the horizon, the towers of the city floated unreal as a dream. The very sky was tinged with blood to his misted glare. He licked his blackened lips and stared with bloodshot eyes at the distant river. It, too, seemed crimson like blood, and the shadows crawling up from the east seemed black as ebony.

In his dulled ears sounded the louder beat of wings. Lifting his head he watched with the burning glare of a wolf the shadows wheeling above him. He knew that his shouts would frighten them away no longer. One dipped —dipped—lower and lower. Conan drew his head back as far as he could, waiting with terrible patience. The vulture swept in with a swift roar of wings. Its beak flashed down, ripping the skin on Conan's chin as he jerked his head aside; then, before the bird could flash away, Conan's head lunged forward on his mighty neck muscles, and his teeth, snapping like those of a wolf, locked on the bare, wattled neck.

Instantly, the vulture exploded into squaking, flapping hysteria. Its thrashing wings blinded the man, and its talons ripped his chest. But grimly he hung on, the muscles starting out in lumps on his jaws. And the scavenger's neck-bones crunched between those powerful teeth. With a spasmodic flutter the bird hung limp. Conan let go, spat blood from his mouth. The other vultures, terrified by the fate of their companion, were in full flight to a distant tree, where they perched like black demons in conclave.

Ferocious triumph surged through Conan's numbed brain. Life beat strongly and savagely through his veins. He could still deal death; he still lived. Every twinge of sensation, even of agony, was a negation of death.

"By Mitra!" Either a voice spoke, or he suffered from hallucination. "In all my life I have never seen such a thing!"

Shaking the sweat and blood from his eyes, Conan saw four horsemen sitting their steeds in the twilight and staring up at him. Three were lean, white-robed hawks, Zuagir tribesmen without a doubt, nomads from beyond the river. The other was dressed like them in a white, girdled khalat and a flowing headdress which, banded about the temples with a triple circlet of braided camel-hair, fell to his shoulders. But he was not a Shemite. The dusk was not so thick, nor Conan's hawklike sight so clouded, that he could not perceive the man's facial characteristics.

He was as tall as Conan, though not so heavy-limbed. His shoulders were broad, and his supple figure was hard as steel and whalebone. A short black beard did not altogether mask the aggressive jut of his lean jaw, and gray eyes cold and piercing as a sword gleamed from the shadow of the kaffia. Quieting his restless steed with a quick, sure hand, this man spoke: "By Mitra, I should know this man!"

"Aye!" It was the guttural accents of a Zuagir. "It is the Cimmerian who was captain of the queen's guard!"

"She must be casting off all her old favorites,"

186

muttered the rider. "Who'd have ever thought it of Queen Taramis? I'd rather have had a long, bloody war. It would have given us desert folk a chance to plunder. As it is, we've come this close to the walls and found only this nag"—he glanced at a fine gelding led by one of the nomads—"and this dying dog."

Conan lifted his bloody head.

"If I could come down from this beam I'd make a dying dog out of you, you Zaporoskan thief!" he rasped through blackened lips.

"Mitra, the knave knows me!" exclaimed the other. "How, knave, do you know me?"

"There's only one of your breed in these parts," muttered Conan. "You are Olgerd Vladislav, the outlaw chief."

"Aye! and once a hetman of the kozaki of the Zaporoskan River, as you have guessed. Would you like to live?"

"Only a fool would ask that question," panted Conan.

"I am a hard man," said Olgerd, "and toughness is the only quality I respect in a man. I shall judge if you are a man, or only a dog after all, fit only to lie here and die."

"If we cut him down we may be seen from the walls," objected one of the nomads.

Olgerd shook his head.

"The dusk is too deep. Here, take this ax, Djebal, and cut down the cross at the base."

"If it falls forward it will crush him," objected Djebal. "I can cut it so it will fall backward, but then the shock of the fall may crack his skull and tear loose all his entrails."

"If he's worthy to ride with me he'll survive it," answered Olgerd imperturbably. "If not, then he doesn't deserve to live. Cut!"

The first impact of the battle-ax against the wood and

its accompanying vibrations sent lances of agony through Conan's swollen feet and hands. Again and again the blade fell, and each stroke reverberated on his bruised brain, setting his tortured nerves aquiver. But he set his teeth and made no sound. The ax cut through, the cross reeled on its splintered base and toppled backward. Conan made his whole body a solid knot of iron-hard muscle, jammed his head back hard against the wood and held it rigid there. The beam struck the ground heavily and rebounded slightly. The impact tore his wounds and dazed him for an instant. He fought the rushing tide of blackness, sick and dizzy, but realized that the iron muscles that sheathed his vitals had saved him from permanent injury.

And he had made no sound, though blood oozed from his nostrils and his belly muscles quivered with nausea. With a grunt of approval, Djebal bent over him with a pair of pincers used to draw horseshoe nails and gripped the head of the spike in Conan's right hand, tearing the skin to get a grip on the deeply embedded head. The pincers were small for that work. Djebal sweated and tugged, swearing and wrestling with the stubborn iron, working it back and forth—in swollen flesh as well as in wood. Blood started, oozing over the Cimmerian's fingers. He lay so still he might have been dead, except for the spasmodic rise and fall of his great chest. The spike gave way, and Djebal held up the bloodstained thing with a grunt of satisfaction, then flung it away and bent over the other.

The process was repeated, and then Djebal turned his attention to Conan's skewered feet. But the Cimmerian, struggling up to a sitting posture, wrenched the pincers from his fingers and sent him staggering backward with a violent shove. Conan's hands were swollen to almost twice their normal size. His fingers felt like misshapen thumbs, and closing his hands was an agony that brought blood streaming from under his grinding teeth. But somehow, clutching the pincers clumsily with both hands, he managed to wrench out first one spike and then the other. They were not driven so deeply into the wood as the others had been.

He rose stiffly and stood upright on his swollen, lacerated feet, swaying drunkenly, the icy sweat dripping from his face and body. Cramps assailed him, and he clamped his jaw against the desire to retch.

Olgerd, watching him impersonally, motioned him toward the stolen horse. Conan stumbled toward it, and every step was a stabbing, throbbing hell that flecked his lips with bloody foam. One misshapen, groping hand fell clumsily on the saddle bow, a bloody foot somehow found the stirrup. Setting his teeth, he swung up, and he almost fainted in midair; but he came down in the saddle—and as he did so, Olgerd struck the horse sharply with his whip. The startled beast reared, and the man in the saddle swayed and slumped like a sack of sand, almost unseated. Conan had wrapped a rein about each hand, holding it in place with a clamping thumb. Drunkenly he exerted the strength of his knotted biceps, wrenching the horse down; it screamed, its jaw almost dislocated.

One of the Shemites lifted a water flask questioningly. Olgerd shook his head.

"Let him wait until we get to camp. It's only ten miles. If he's fit to live in the desert, he'll live that long without a drink."

The group rode like swift ghosts toward the river; among them Conan swayed like a drunken man in the saddle, bloodshot eyes glazed, foam drying on his blackened lips.

### 3. *A Letter to Nemedia*

The savant Astreas, traveling in the East in his never-tiring search for knowledge, wrote a letter to his friend and fellow philosopher Alcemides, in his native Nemedia, which constitutes the entire knowledge of the western nations concerning the events of that period in the east, always a hazy, half-mythical region in the minds of the western folk.

Astreas wrote, in part: "You can scarcely conceive, my dear old friend, of the conditions now existing in this tiny kingdom since Queen Taramis admitted Constantius and his mercenaries, an event which I briefly described in my last, hurried letter. Seven months have passed since then, during which time it seems as though the Devil himself had been loosed in this unfortunate realm. Taramis seems to have gone quite mad; whereas formerly she was famed for her virtue, justice, and tranquality, she is now notorious for qualities precisely opposite to those just enumerated. Her private life is a scandal—or perhaps 'private' is not the correct term, since the queen makes no attempt to conceal the debauchery of her court. She constantly indulges in the most infamous revelries, in which the unfortunate ladies of the court are forced to join, young married women as well as virgins.

"She herself has not bothered to marry her paramour, Constantius, who sits on the throne beside her and reigns as her royal consort, and his officers follow his example and do not hesitate to debauch any woman they desire, regardless of her rank or station. The wretched kingdom groans under exorbitant taxation, the farms are stripped to the bone, and the merchants go in rags, which are all that is left them by the tax gatherers. Nay, they are lucky if they escape with a whole skin.

"I sense your incredulity, good Alcemides; you will fear that I exaggerate conditions in Khauran. Such conditions would be unthinkable in any of the western countries, admittedly. But you must realize the vast difference that exists between west and east, especially this part of the east. In the first place, Khauran is a kingdom of no great size, one of the many principalities which at one time formed the eastern part of the empire of Koth, and which later regained the independence which was theirs at a still earlier age. This part of the world is made up of these tiny realms, diminutive in comparison with the great kingdoms of the west, or the great sultanates of the farther east, but important in their control of the caravan routes and in the wealth concentrated in them.

"Khauran is the most southeasterly of these principalities, bordering on the very deserts of eastern Shem. The city of Khauran is the only city of any magnitude in the realm and stands within sight of the river which separates the grasslands from the sandy desert, like a watchtower to guard the fertile meadows behind it. The land is so rich that it yields three and four crops a year, and the plains north and west of the city are dotted with villages. To one accustomed to the great plantations and stock farms of the west, it is strange to see these tiny fields and vineyards; yet wealth in grain and fruit pours from them as from a horn of plenty. The villagers are agriculturists, nothing else. Of a mixed, aboriginal race, they are unwarlike, unable to protect themselves, and forbidden the possession of arms. Dependent wholly upon the soldiers of the city for protection, they are helpless under the present conditions. So the savage revolt of the rural sections, which would be a certainty in any western nation, is here impossible.

"They toil supinely under the iron hand of Constantius, and his black-bearded Shemites ride incessantly through the fields with whips in their hands like the slave drivers of the black serfs who toil in the plantations of southern Zingara.

"Nor do the people of the city fare any better. Their wealth is stripped from them, their fairest daughters taken to glut the insatiable lust of Constantius and his mercenaries. These men are utterly without mercy or compassion, possessed of all the characteristics our armies learned to abhor in our wars against the Shemitish allies of Argos—inhuman cruelty, lust, and wild-beast ferocity. The people of the city are Khauran's ruling caste, predominantly Hyborian, and valorous and warlike. But the treachery of their queen delivered them into the hands of their oppressors. The Shemites are the only armed force in Khauran, and the most hellish punishment is inflicted on any Khauran found possessing weapons. A systematic persecution to destroy the young Khaurani men able to bear arms has been savagely pursued. Many have ruthlessly been slaughtered, others sold as slaves to the Turanians. Thousands have fled the kingdom and either entered the service of other rulers, or become outlaws, lurking in numerous bands along the borders.

"At present there is some possibility of invasion from the desert, which is inhabited by tribes of Shemitish nomads. The mercenaries of Constantius are men from the Shemitish cities of the west, Pelishtim, Anakim, Akkharim, and are ardently hated by the Zuagirs and other wandering tribes. As you know, good Alcemides, the countries of these barbarians are divided into the western meadowlands which stretch to the distant ocean, and in which rise the cities of the town-dwellers, and the eastern deserts, where the lean nomads hold sway; there is incessant warfare between the dwellers of the cities and the dwellers of the desert.

192

"The Zuagirs have fought with and raided Khauran for centuries without success, but they resent its conquest by their western kin. It is rumored that their natural antagonism is being fometed by the man who was formerly the captain of the queen's guard, and who, somehow escaping the hate of Constantius, who actually had him upon the cross, fled to the nomads. He is called Conan, and is himself a barbarian, one of those gloomy Cimmerians whose ferocity our soldiers have more than once learned to their bitter cost. It is rumored that he has become the right-hand man of Olgerd Vladislav, the kozak adventurer who wandered down from the northern steppes and made himself chief of a band of Zuagirs. There are also rumors that this band has increased vastly in the last few months, and that Olgerd, incited no doubt by this Cimmerian, is even considering a raid on Khauran.

"It cannot be anything more than a raid, as the Zuagirs are without siege machines or the knowledge of taking a city, and it has been proved repeatedly in the past that the nomads in their loose formation, or rather lack of formation, are no match in hand-to-hand fighting for the well-disciplined, fully armed warriors of the Shemitish cities. The natives of Khauran would perhaps welcome this conquest, since the nomads could deal with them no more harshly than their present masters, and even total extermination would be preferable to the suffering they have to endure. But they are so cowed and helpless that they could give no aid to the invaders.

"Their plight is most wretched. Taramis, apparently possessed of a demon, stops at nothing. She has abolished the worship of Ishtar and turned the temple into a shrine of idolatry. She has destroyed the ivory image of the goddess which these eastern Hyborians worship (and which, inferior as it is to the true religion of Mitra which we Western nations recognize, is still superior to the devil worship of the Shemites) and filled the temple of Ishtar

193

with obscene images of every imaginable sort—gods and goddesses of the night, portrayed in all the salacious and perverse poses and with all the revolting characteristics that a degenerate brain could conceive. Many of these images are to be identified as foul deities of the Shemites, the Turanians, the Vendhyans, and the Khitans, but others are reminiscent of a hideous and half-remembered antiquity, vile shapes forgotten except in the most obscure legends. Where the queen gained the knowledge of them I dare not even hazard a guess.

"She has instituted human sacrifice, and since her mating with Constantius, no less than five hundred men, women, and children have been immolated. Some of these have died on the altar she has set up in the temple, herself wielding the sacrificial dagger, but most have met a more horrible doom.

"Taramis has placed some sort of monster in a crypt in the temple. What it is, and whence it came, none knows. But shortly after she had crushed the desperate revolt of her soldiers against Constantius, she spent a night alone in the desecrated temple, alone except for a dozen bound captives, and the shuddering people saw thick, foul-smelling smoke curling up from the dome, heard all night the frenetic chanting of the queen, and the agonized cries of her tortured captives; and toward dawn another voice mingled wih these sounds—a strident, inhuman croaking that froze the blood of all who heard.

"In the full dawn, Taramis reeled drunkenly from the temple, her eyes blazing with demoniac triumph. The captives were never seen again, nor the croaking voice heard. But there is a room in the temple into which none ever goes but the queen, driving a human sacrifice before her. And this victim is never seen again. All know that in that grim chamber lurks some monster from the black night of ages, which devours the shrieking humans Taramis delivers up to it.

194

"I can no longer think of her as a mortal woman, but as a rabid she-fiend, crouching in her blood-fouled lair amongst the bones and fragments of her victims, with taloned, crimsoned fingers. That the gods allow her to pursue her awful course unchecked almost shakes my faith in divine justice.

"When I compare her present conduct with her deportment when first I came to Khauran, seven months ago, I am confused with bewilderment, and almost inclined to the belief held by the people—that a demon has possessed the body of Taramis. A young soldier, Valerius, had another belief. He believed that a witch had assumed a form identical with that of Khauran's adored ruler. He believed that Taramis had been spirited away in the night and confined in some dungeon, and that this being ruling in her place was but a female sorcerer. He swore that he would find the real queen, if she still lived, but I greatly fear that he himself has fallen victim to the cruelty of Constantius. He was implicated in the revolt of the palace guards, escaped, and remained in hiding for some time, stubbornly refusing to seek safety abroad, and it was during this time that I encountered him and he told me his beliefs.

"But he has disappeared, as so many have, whose fate one dares not conjecture, and I fear he has been apprehended by the spies of Constantius.

"But I must conclude this letter and slip it out of the city by means of a swift carrier pigeon, which will carry it to the post whence I purchased it, on the borders of Koth. By rider and camel train it will eventually come to you. I must haste, before dawn. It is late, and the stars gleam whitely on the gardened roofs of Kahuran. A shuddering silence envelops the city, in which I hear the throb of a sullen drum from the distant temple. I doubt not that Taramis is there, concocting more deviltry."

195

But the savant was incorrect in his conjecture concerning the whereabouts of the woman he called Taramis. The girl whom the world knew as queen of Khauran stood in a dungeon, lighted only by a flickering torch which played on her features, etching the diabolical cruelty of her beautiful countenance.

On the bare stone floor before her crouched a figure whose nakedness was scarcely covered with tattered rags.

This figure Salome touched contemptuously with the upturned toe of her gilded sandal, and smiled vindictively as her victim shrank away.

"You do not love my caresses, sweet sister?"

Taramis was still beautiful, in spite of her rags and the imprisonment and abuse of seven weary months. She did not reply to her sister's taunts, but bent her head as one grown accustomed to mockery.

This resignation did not please Salome. She bit her red lip, and stood tapping the toe of her shoe against the flags as she frowned down at the passive figure. Salome was clad in the barbaric splendor of a woman of Shushan. Jewels glittered in the torchlight on her gilded sandals, on her gold breast-plates and the slender chains that held them in place. Gold anklets clashed as she moved, jeweled bracelets weighted her bare arms. Her tall coiffure was that of a Shemitish woman, and jade pendants hung from gold hoops in her ears, flashing and sparkling with each impatient movement of her haughty head. A gem-crusted girdle supported a silk skirt so transparent that it was in the nature of a cynical mockery of convention.

Suspended from her shoulders and trailing down her back hung a darkly scarlet cloak, and this was thrown carelessly over the crook of one arm and the bundle that arm supported.

Salome stooped suddenly and with her free hand grasped her sister's disheveled hair and forced back the girl's head to stare into her eyes. Taramis met that tigerish glare without flinching.

"You are not so ready with your tears as formerly, sweet sister," muttered the witch-girl.

"You shall wring no more tears from me," answered Taramis. "Too often you have reveled in the spectacle of the queen of Khauran sobbing for mercy on her knees. I know that you have spared me only to torment me; that is why you have limited your tortures to such torments as neither slay nor permanently disfigure. But I fear you no longer; you have strained out the last vestige of hope, fright, and shame from me. Slay me and be done with it, for I have shed my last tear for your enjoyment, you she-devil from Hell!"

"You flatter yourself, my dear sister," purred Salome. "So far it is only your handsome body that I have caused to suffer, only your pride and self-esteem that I have crushed. You forget that, unlike myself, you are capable of mental torment. I have observed this when I have regaled you with narratives concerning the comedies I have enacted with some of your stupid subjects. But this time I have brought more vivid proof of these farces. Did you know that Krallides, your faithful councillor, had come sulking back from Turan and been captured?"

Taramis turned pale.

"What—what have you done to him?"

For answer Salome drew the mysterious bundle from under her cloak. She shook off the silken swathings and held it up—the head of a young man, the features frozen in a convulsion as if death had come in the midst of in-human agony.

Taramis cried out as if a blade had pierced her heart.

"Oh, Ishtar! Krallides!"

"Aye! He was seeking to stir up the people against me, poor fool, telling them that Conan spoke the truth when he said I was not Taramis. How would the people rise against the Falcon's Shemites? With sticks and pebbles? Bah! Dogs are eating his headless body in the market place, and this foul carrion shall be cast into the sewer to rot.

"How, sister!" She paused, smiling down at her victim. "Have you discovered that you still have unshed tears? Good! I reserved the mental torment for the last. Hereafter I shall show you many such sights as—this!"

Standing there in the torchlight with the severed head in her hand she did not look like anything ever born of a human woman, in spite of her awful beauty. Taramis did not look up. She lay face down on the slimy floor, her slim body shaken in sobs of agony, beating her clenched hands against the stones. Salome sauntered toward the door, her anklets clashing at each step, her ear pendants winking in the torch-glare.

A few moments later, she emerged from a door under a sullen arch that let into a court, which in turn opened upon a winding alley. A man standing there turned toward her—a giant Shemite, with somber eyes and shoulders like a bull, his great black beard falling over his mighty, silver-mailed breast.

"She wept?" His rumble was like that of a bull, deep, low-pitched, and stormy. He was the general of the mercenaries, one of the few even of Constantius' associates who knew the secret of the queen of Khauran.

"Aye, Khumbanigash. There are whole sections of her sensibilities that I have not touched. When one sense is dulled by continual laceration, I will discover a newer, more poignant pang.—Here, dog!" A trembling, shambling figure in rags, filth, and matted hair approached, one of the beggars that slept in the alleys and open courts. Salome tossed the head to him. "Here, deaf one; cast that in the nearest sewer.—Make the sign with your hands, Khumbanigash. He cannot hear."

198

The general complied, and the tousled head bobbed, as the man turned painfully away.

"Why do you keep up this farce?" rumbled Khumbanigash. "You are so firmly established on the throne that nothing can unseat you. What if the Khaurani fools learn the truth? They can do nothing. Proclaim yourself in your true identity! Show them their beloved ex-queen —and cut off her head in the public square!"

"Not yet, good Khumbanigash——"

The arched door slammed on the hard accents of Salome, the stormy reverberations of Khumbanigash. The mute beggar crouched in the courtyard, and there was none to see that the hands which held the severed head were quivering strongly—brown, sinewy hands, strangely incongruous with the bent body and filthy tatters.

"I knew it!" It was a fierce, vibrant whisper, scarcely audible. "She lives! Oh, Krallides, your martyrdom was not in vain! They have her locked in that dungeon! Oh, Ishtar, if you love true men, aid me now!"

## 4. *Wolves of the Desert*

Olgerd Vladislav filled his jeweled goblet with crimson wine from a golden jug and thrust the vessel across the ebony table to Conan the Cimmerian. Olgerd's apparel would have satisfied the vanity of any Zaporoskan hetman.

His *khalat* was of white silk, with pearls sewn on the bosom. Girdled at the waist with a Bakhauriot belt, its skirts were drawn back to reveal his wide silken breeches, tucked into short boots of soft green leather, adorned with gold thread. On his head was a green silk turban, wound about a spired helmet chased with gold. His only weapon was a broad curved Cherkees knife in an ivory sheath girdled high on his left hip, *kozak* fashion. Throwing himself back in his gilded chair with its carven eagles, Olgerd spread his booted legs before him and gulped down the sparkling wine noisily.

To his splendor the huge Cimmerian opposite him offered a strong contrast, with his square-cut black mane, brown, scarred countenance and burning blue eyes. He was clad in black mesh mail, and the only glitter about him was the broad gold buckle of the belt which supported his sword in its worn leather scabbard.

They were alone in the silk-walled tent, which was hung with gild-worked tapestries and littered with rich carpets and velvet cushions, the loot of the caravans. From outside came a low, incessant murmur, the sound that always accompanies a great throng of men, in camp or otherwise. An occasional gust of desert wind rattled the palm leaves.

"Today in the shadow, tomorrow in the sun," quoth Olgerd, loosening his crimson girdle a trifle and reaching again for the wine jug. "That's the way of life. Once I was a hetman on the Zaporoska; now I'm a desert chief. Seven months ago you were hanging on a cross outside Khauran. Now you're lieutenant to the most powerful raider between Turan and the western meadows. You should be thankful to me!"

"For recognizing my usefulness?" Conan laughed and lifted the jug. "When you allow the elevation of a man, one can be sure that you'll profit by his advancement. I've earned everything I've won, with my blood and sweat." He glanced at the scars on the insides of his palms. There were scars, too, on his body, scars that had not been there seven months ago.

"You fight like a regiment of devils," conceded Olgerd. "But don't get to thinking that you've had anything to do with the recruits who've swarmed in to join us. It was our success at raiding, guided by my wit, that brought

200

them in. These nomads are always looking for a success-ful leader to follow, and they have more faith in a for-eigner than in one of their own race.

"There's no limit to what we may accomplish! We have eleven thousand men now. In another year we may have three times that number. We've contented ourselves, so far, with raids on the Turanian outposts and the city-states to the west. With thirty or forty thousand men we'll raid no longer. We'll invade and conquer and estab-lish ourselves as rulers. I'll be emperor of all Shem yet, and you'll be my vizier, so long as you carry out my or-ders unquestioningly. In the meantime, I think we'll ride eastward and storm that Turanian outpost at Vezek, where the caravans pay toll."

Conan shook his head. "I think not."

Olgerd glared, his quick temper irritated.

"What do you mean, *you* think not? *I* do the thinking for this army!"

"There are enough men in this band now for my pur-pose," answered the Cimmerian. "I'm sick of waiting. I have a score to settle."

"Oh!" Olgerd scowled, and gulped wine, then grinned. "Still thinking of that cross, eh? Well, I like a good hater. But that can wait."

"You told me once you'd aid me in taking Khauran," said Conan.

"Yes, but that was before I began to see the full possi-bilities of our power," answered Olgerd. "I was only thinking of the loot in the city. I don't want to waste our strength unprofitably. Khauran is too strong a nut for us to crack now. Maybe in a year——"

"Within the week," answered Conan, and the *kozak* started at the certainty in his voice.

"Listen," said Olgerd, "even if I were willing to throw away men on such a harebrained attempt—what could you expect? Do you think these wolves could besiege and take a city like Khauran?"

"There'll be no siege," answered the Cimmerian. "I know how to draw Constantius out into the plain."

"And what then?" cried Olgerd with an oath. "In the arrow play our horsemen would have the worst of it, for the armor of the *asshuri* is the better, and when it came to sword strokes their close-marshaled ranks of trained swordsmen would cleave through our loose lines and scatter our men like chaff before the wind."

"Not if there were three thousand desperate Hyborian horsemen fighting in a solid wedge such as I could teach them," answered Conan.

"And where would you secure three thousand Hyborians?" asked Olgerd with vast sarcasm. "Will you conjure them out of the air?"

"I *have* them," answered the Cimmerian imperturbably. "Three thousand men of Khauran camp at the oasis of Akrel, awaiting my orders."

"*What?*" Olgerd glared like a startled wolf.

"Aye. Men who had fled from the tyranny of Constantius. Most of them have been living the lives of outlaws in the deserts east of Khauran and are gaunt and hard and desperate as man-eating tigers. One of them will be a match for any three squat mercenaries. It takes oppression and hardship to stiffen men's guts and put the fire of Hell into their thews. They were broken up into small bands; all they needed was a leader. They believed the word I sent them by my riders, and assembled at the oasis and put themselves at my disposal."

"All this without my knowledge?" A feral light began to gleam in Olgerd's eyes. He hitched at his weapongirdle.

"It was *I* they wished to follow, not *you*."

"And what did you tell these outcasts to gain their allegiance?" There was a dangerous ring in Olgerd's voice.

"I told them that I'd use this horde of desert wolves to help them destroy Constantius and give Khauran back into the hands of its citizens."

"You fool!" whispered Olgerd. "Do you deem yourself chief already?"

The men were on their feet, facing each other across the ebony board, devil-lights dancing in Olgerd's cold gray eyes, a grim smile on the Cimmerian's hard lips.

"I'll have you torn between four palm trees," said the *kozak* calmly.

"Call the men and bid them do it!" challenged Conan. "See if they obey you!"

Baring his teeth in a snarl, Olgerd lifted his hand—then paused. There was something about the confidence in the Cimmerian's dark face that shook him. His eyes began to burn like those of a wolf.

"You scum of the western hills," he muttered, "have you dared to seek to undermine my power?"

"I didn't have to," answered Conan. "You lied when you said I had nothing to do with bringing in the new recruits. I had everything to do with it. They took your orders, but they fought for me. There is not room for two chiefs of the Zuagirs. They know I am the stronger man. I understand them better than you, and they, me; because I am a barbarian too."

"And what will they say when you ask them to fight for the Khauranis?" asked Olgerd sardonically.

"They'll follow me. I'll promise them a camel train of gold from the palace. Khauran will be willing to pay that as a guerdon for getting rid of Constantius. After that, I'll lead them against the Turanians as you have planned. They want loot, and they'd as soon fight Constantius for it as anybody."

In Olgerd's eyes grew a recognition of defeat. In his red dreams of empire he had missed what was going on about him. Happenings and events that had seemed meaningless before now flashed into his mind, with their true significance, bringing a realization that Conan spoke no idle boast. The giant black-mailed figure before him was the real chief of the Zuagirs.

"Not if you die!" muttered Olgerd, and his hand flickered toward his hilt. But quick as the stroke of a great cat Conan's arm shot across the table and his fingers locked on Olgerd's forearm. There was a snap of breaking bones, and for a tense instant the scene held: the men facing each other as motionless as images, perspiration starting out on Olgerd's forehead. Conan laughed, never easing his grip on the broken arm.

"Are you fit to live, Olgerd?"

His smile did not alter as the corded muscles rippled in knotting ridges along his forearm and his fingers ground into the *kozak*'s quivering flesh. There was the sound of broken bones grating together and Olgerd's face turned the color of ashes; blood oozed from his lip where his teeth sank, but he uttered no sound.

With a laugh Conan released him and drew back, and the *kozak* swayed, caught the table edge with his good hand to steady himself.

"I give you life, Olgerd, as you gave it to me," said Conan tranquilly, "though it was for your own ends that you took me down from the cross. It was a bitter test you gave me then—you couldn't have endured it, nor could anyone but a western barbarian.

"Take your horse and go. It's tied behind the tent, and food and water are in the saddlebags. None will see your going, but go quickly. There's no room for a fallen chief on the desert. If the warriors see you, maimed and deposed, they'll never let you leave the camp alive."

Olgerd did not reply. Slowly, without a word, he turned and stalked across the tent, through the flapped opening. Unspeaking he climbed into the saddle of the great white stallion that stood tethered there in the shade of a spreading palm tree; and unspeaking, with his broken arm thrust in the bosom of his *khalat*, he reined the steed about and rode eastward into the open desert, out of the life of the people of the Zuagir.

Inside the tent Conan emptied the wine jug and smacked his lips with relish. Tossing the empty vessel into a corner, he braced his belt and strode out through the front opening, halting for a moment to let his gaze sweep over the lines of camel-hair tents that stretched before him, and the white-robed figures that moved among them, arguing, singing, mending bridles, or whetting tulwars.

He lifted his voice in a thunder that carried to the farthest confines of the encampment: "*Aie*, you dogs, sharpen your ears and listen! Gather around here. I have a tale to tell you."

## 5. The Voice from the Crystal

In a chamber in a tower near the city wall, a group of men listened attentively to the words of one of their number. They were young men, but hard and sinewy, with the bearing that comes only to men rendered desperate by adversity. They were clad in mail shirts and worn leather; swords hung at their girdles.

"I knew that Conan spoke the truth when he said it was not Taramis!" the speaker exclaimed. "For months I have haunted the outskirts of the palace, playing the part of a deaf beggar. At last I learned what I had believed— that our queen was a prisoner in the dungeons that adjoin the palace. I watched my opportunity and captured a Shemitish jailer—knocked him senseless as he left the courtyard late one night—dragged him into a cellar nearby and questioned him. Before he died, he told me what I have just told you, and what we have suspected all along—that the woman ruling Khauran is a witch: Salome. Taramis, he said, is imprisoned in the lowest dungeon.

"This invasion of the Zuagirs gives us the opportunity we sought. What Conan means to do, I cannot say. Perhaps he merely wishes vengeance on Constantius. Perhaps he intends sacking the city and destroying it. He is a barbarian, and no one can understand their minds.

"But this is what we must do: rescue Taramis while the battle rages! Constantius will march out into the plain to give battle. Even now his men are mounting. He will do this because there is not sufficient food in the city to stand a siege. Conan burst out of the desert so suddenly that there was no time to bring supplies. And the Cimmerian is equipped for a siege. Scouts have reported that the Zuagirs have siege engines, built, undoubtedly, according to the instructions of Conan, who learned all the arts of war among the Western nations.

"Constantius does not desire a long siege; so he will march with his warriors into the plain, where he expects to scatter Conan's forces at one stroke. He will leave only a few hundred men in the city, and they will be on the walls and in the towers commanding the gates.

"The prison will be left all but unguarded. When we have freed Taramis, our next actions will depend upon circumstances. If Conan wins, we must show Taramis to the people and bid them rise—they will! Oh, they will! With their bare hands they are enough to overpower the Shemites left in the city and close the gates against both the mercenaries and the nomads. Neither must get within the walls! Then we will parley with Conan. He was always loyal to Taramis. If he knows the truth, and she appeals to him, I believe he will spare the city. If, which is more probable, Constantius prevails, and Conan is routed, we must steal out of the city with the queen and seek safety in flight.

"Is all clear?"

They replied with one voice.

"Then let us loosen our blades in our scabbards, commend our souls to Ishtar, and start for the prison, for the mercenaries are already marching through the southern gate."

This was true. The dawnlight glinted on peaked helmets pouring in a steady stream through the broad arch, on the bright housings of the chargers. This would be a battle of horsemen, such as is possible only in the lands of the east. The riders flowed through the gates like a river of steel—somber figures in black and silver mail, with their curled beards and hooked noses, and their inexorable eyes in which glimmered the fatality of their race—the utter lack of doubt or of mercy.

The streets and the walls were lined with throngs of people who watched silently these warriors of an alien race riding forth to defend their native city. There was no sound; dully, expressionlessly they watched, those gaunt people in shabby garments, their caps in their hands.

In a tower that overlooked the broad street that led to the southern gate, Salome lolled on a velvet couch, cynically watching Constantius as he settled his broad sword belt about his lean hips and drew on his gauntlets. They were alone in the chamber. Outside, the rhythmical clank of harness and shuffle of horses' hooves welled up through the gold-barred casements.

"Before nightfall," quoth Constantius, giving a twirl to is thin mustache, "you'll have some captives to feed to your temple devil. Does it not grow weary of soft, city-bred flesh? Perhaps it would relish the harder thews of a desert man."

"Take care you do not fall prey to a fiercer beast than

207

Thaug," warned the girl. "Do not forget who it is that leads these desert animals."

"I am not likely to forget," he answered. "That is one reason why I am advancing to meet him. The dog has fought in the west and knows the art of siege. My scouts had some trouble in approaching his columns, for his outriders have eyes like hawks; but they did get close enough to see the engines he is dragging on oxcart wheels drawn by camels—catapults, rams, ballistas, mangonels—by Ishtar! he must have had ten thousand men working day and night for a month. Where he got the material for their construction is more than I can understand. Perhaps he has a treaty with the Turanians and gets supplies from them.

"Anyway, they won't do him any good. I've fought these desert wolves before—an exchange of arrows for a while, in which the armor of my warriors protects them—then a charge and my squadrons sweep through the loose swarms of the nomads, wheel and sweep back through, scattering them to the four winds. I'll ride back through the south gate before sunset, with hundreds of naked captives staggering at my horse's tail. We'll hold a fête tonight, in the great square. My soldiers delight in flaying their enemies alive—we will have a wholesale skinning, and make these weak-kneed townsfolk watch. As for Conan, it will afford me intense pleasure, if we can take him alive, to impale him on the palace steps."

"Skin as many as you like," answered Salome indifferently. "I would like a dress made of human hide. But at least a hundred captives you must give to me—for the altar, and for Thaug."

"It shall be done," answered Constantius, with his gauntleted hand brushing back the thin hair from his high, bald forehead, burned dark by the sun. "For victory and the fair honor of Taramis!" he said sardonically, and, taking his visored helmet under his arm, he lifted a hand in salute and strode clanking from the chamber. His voice drifted back, harshly lifted in orders to his officers.

Salome leaned back on the couch, yawned, stretched herself like a great, supple cat, and called: "Zang!"

A cat-footed priest, with features like yellowed parchment stretched over a skull, entered noiselessly.

Salome turned to an ivory pedestal on which stood two crystal globes and, taking from it the smaller, she handed the glistening sphere to the priest.

"Ride with Constantius," she said. "Give me the news of the battle. Go!"

The skull-faced man bowed low and, hiding the globe under his dark mantle, hurried from the chamber.

Outside in the city there was no sound, except the clank of hoofs and after a while the clang of a closing gate. Salome mounted a wide marble stair that led to the flat, canopied, marble-battlemented roof. She was above all other buildings of the city. The streets were deserted, the great square in front of the palace was empty. In normal times folk shunned the grim temple which rose on the opposite side of that square, but now the town looked like a dead city. Only on the southern wall and the roofs that overlooked it was there any sign of life. There the people massed thickly. They made no demonstration, did not know whether to hope for the victory or defeat of Constantius. Victory meant further misery under his intolerable rule; defeat probably meant the sack of the city and red massacre. No word had come from Conan. They did not know what to expect at his hands. They remembered that he was a barbarian.

The squadrons of the mercenaries were moving out into the plain. In the distance, just this side of the river, other dark masses were moving, barely recognizable as men on horses. Objects dotted the farther bank; Conan had not brought his siege engines across the river, apparently fearing an attack in the midst of the crossing. But he had crossed with his full force of horsemen. The sun rose and struck glints of fire from the dark multitudes. The squadrons from the city broke into a gallop; a deep roar reached the ears of the people on the wall.

The rolling masses merged, intermingled; at that distance it was a tangled confusion in which no details stood out. Charge and countercharge were not to be identified. Clouds of dust rose from the plains, under the stamping hoofs, veiling the action. Through these swirling clouds masses of riders loomed, appearing and disappearing, and spears flashed.

Salome shrugged her shoulders and descended the stair. The palace lay silent. All the slaves were on the wall, gazing vainly southward with the citizens.

She entered the chamber where she had talked with Constantius and approached the pedestal, noting that the crystal globe was clouded, shot with bloody streaks of crimson. She bent over the ball, swearing under her breath.

"Zang!" she called. "Zang!"

Mists swirled in the sphere, resolving themselves into billowing dust clouds through which black figures rushed unrecognizably; steel glinted like lightning in the murk. Then the face of Zang leaped into startling distinctness; it was as if the wide eyes gazed up at Salome. Blood trickled from a gash in the skull-like head, the skin was gray with sweat-runneled dust. The lips parted, writhing; to other ears than Salome's it would have seemed that the face in the crystal contorted silently. But sound to her came as plainly from those ashen lips as if the priest had been in the same room with her, instead of miles away, shouting into the smaller crystal. Only the gods of darkness knew what unseen, magic filaments linked together those shimmering spheres.

"Salome!" shrieked the bloody head. "*Salome!*"

"I hear!" she cried. "Speak! How goes the battle?"

"Doom is upon us!" screamed the skull-like apparition.

"Khauran is lost! *Aie*, my horse is down and I cannot win clear! Men are falling around me! They are dying like flies, in their silvered mail!"

"Stop yammering and tell me what happened!" she cried harshly.

"We rode at the desert dogs, and they came on to meet us!" yowled the priest. "Arrows flew in clouds between the hosts, and the nomads wavered. Constantius ordered the charge. In even ranks we thundered upon them.

"Then the masses of their horde opened to right and left, and through the cleft rushed three thousand Hyborian horsemen whose presence we had not even suspected. Men of Khauran, mad with hate! Big men in full armor on massive horses! In a solid wedge of steel they smote us like a thunderbolt. They split our ranks asunder before we knew what was upon us, and then the desert men swarmed on us from either flank.

"They have ripped our ranks apart, broken and scattered us! It is a trick of that devil Conan! The siege engines are false—mere frames of palm trunks and painted silk, that fooled our scouts who saw them from afar. A trick to draw us out to our doom! Our warriors flee! Khumbanigash is down—Conan slew him. I do not see Constantius. The Khauranis rage through our milling masses like blood-mad lions, and the desert men feather us with arrows. I—ahhh!"

There was a flicker as of lightning, or trenchant steel, a burst of bright blood—then abruptly the image vanished, like a bursting bubble, and Salome was staring into an empty crystal ball that mirrored only her own furious features.

She stood perfectly still for a few moments, erect and staring into space. Then she clapped her hands and another skull-like priest entered, as silent and immobile as the first.

"Constantius is beaten," she said swiftly. "We are

211

doomed. Conan will be crashing at our gates within the hour. If he catches me, I have no illusions as to what I can expect. But first I am going to make sure that my cursed sister never ascends the throne again. Follow me! Come what may, we shall give Thaug a feast."

As she descended the stairs and galleries of the palace, she heard a faint, rising echo from the distant walls. The people there had begun to realize that the battle was going against Constantius. Through the dust clouds masses of horsemen were visible, racing toward the city.

Palace and prison were connected by a long closed gallery, whose vaulted roof rose on gloomy arches. Hurrying along this, the false queen and her slave passed through a heavy door at the other end that let them into the dim-lit recesses of the prison. They had emerged into a wide, arched corridor at a point near where a stone stair descended into the darkness. Salome recoiled suddenly, swearing. In the gloom of the hall lay a motionless form —a Shemitish jailer, his short beard tilted toward the roof as his head hung on a half-severed neck. As panting voices from below reached the girl's ears, she shrank back into the black shadow of an arch, pushing the priest behind her, her hand groping in her girdle.

## 6. The Vulture's Wings

It was the smoky light of a torch which roused Taramis, queen of Khauran, from the slumber in which she sought forgetfulness. Lifting herself on her hand, she raked back her tangled hair and blinked up, expecting to meet the mocking countenance of Salome, malign with new torments. Instead a cry of pity and horror reached her ears.

212

"Taramis! Oh, my queen!"

The sound was so strange to her ears that she thought she was still dreaming. Behind the torch she could make out figures now, the glint of steel, then five countenances bent toward her, not swarthy and hook-nosed, but lean, aquiline faces, browned by the sun. She crouched in her tatters, staring wildly.

One of the figures sprang forward and fell on one knee before her, arms stretched appealingly toward her.

"Oh, Taramis! Thank Ishtar we have found you! Do you not remember me, Valerius? Once with your own lips you praised me, after the battle of Korveka!"

"Valerius!" she stammered. Suddenly tears welled into her eyes. "Oh, I dream! It is some magic of Salome's, to torment me!"

"No!" The cry rang with exultation. "It is your own true vassals come to rescue you! Yet we must hasten. Constantius fights in the plain against Conan, who has brought the Zuagirs across the river, but three hundred Shemites yet hold the city. We slew the jailer and took his keys, and have seen no other guards. But we must be gone. Come!"

The queen's legs gave way, not from weakness but from emotion. Valerius lifted her like a child, and with the torchbearer hurrying before them, they left the dungeon and went up a slimy stone stair. It seemed to mount endlessly, but presently they emerged into a corridor.

They were passing a dark arch when the torch was suddenly struck out, and the bearer cried out in fierce, brief agony. A burst of blue fire glared in the dark corridor, in which the furious face of Salome was limned momentarily, with a beastlike figure crouching beside her —then the eyes of the watchers were blinded by that blaze.

Valerius tried to stagger along the corridor with the queen; dazedly he heard the sound of murderous blows

213

driven deep in flesh, accompanied by gasps of death and a bestial grunting. Then the queen was torn brutally from his arms, and a savage blow on his helmet dashed him to the floor.

Grimly he crawled to his feet, shaking his head in an effort to rid himself of the blue flame, which seemed still to dance devilishly before him. When his blinded sight cleared, he found himself alone in the corridor—alone except for the dead. His four companions lay in their blood, heads and bosoms cleft and gashed. Blinded and dazed in that hell-born glare, they had died without an opportunity of defending themselves. The queen was gone.

With a bitter curse Valerius caught up his sword, tearing his cleft helmet from his head to clatter on the flags; blood ran down his cheek from a cut in his scalp.

Reeling, frantic with indecision, he heard a voice calling his name in desperate urgency: "Valerius! Valerius!"

He staggered in the direction of the voice, and rounded a corner just in time to have his arms filled with a soft, supple figure which flung itself frantically at him.

"Ivga! Are you mad!"

"I had to come!" she sobbed. "I followed you—hid in an arch of the outer court. A moment ago I saw *her* emerge with a brute who carried a woman in his arms. I knew it was Taramis, and that you had failed! Oh, you are hurt!"

"A scratch!" He put aside her clinging hands. "Quick, Ivga, tell me which way they went!"

"They fled across the square toward the temple."

He paled. "Ishtar! Oh, the fiend! She means to give Taramis to the devil she worships! Quick, Ivga! Run to the south wall where the people watch the battle! Tell them that their real queen has been found—that the imposter has dragged her to the temple! Go!"

214

Sobbing, the girl sped away, her light sandals pattering across the court, plunged into the street, dashed into the square upon which it debouched, and raced for the great structure that rose on the opposite side.

His own flying feet spurned the marble as he darted up the broad stair and through the pillared portico. Evidently their prisoner had given them some trouble. Taramis, sensing the doom intended for her, was fighting against it with all the strength of her splendid young body. Once she had broken away from the brutish priest, only to be dragged down again.

The group was half way down the broad nave, at the other end of which stood the grim altar and beyond that the great metal door, obscenely carven, through which many had gone but from which only Salome had ever emerged. Taramis' breath came in panting gasps; her tattered garment had been torn from her in the struggle. She writhed in the grasp of her apish captor like a white, naked nymph in the arms of a satyr. Salome watched cynically, though impatiently, moving toward the carven door; and from the dusk that lurked along the lofty walls the obscene gods and gargoyles leered down, as if imbued with salacious life.

Choking with fury, Valerius rushed down the great hall, sword in hand. At a sharp cry from Salome, the skull-faced priest looked up, then released Taramis, drew a heavy knife, already smeared with blood, and ran at the oncoming Khaurani.

But cutting down men blinded by the devil's flame loosed by Salome was different from fighting a wiry young Hyborian afire with hate and rage.

Up went the dripping knife, but before it could fall Valerius' keen narrow blade slashed through the air, and the fist that held the knife jumped from its wrist in a shower of blood. Valerius, berserk, slashed again and yet again before the crumpling figure could fall. The blade licked through flesh and bone. The skull-like head fell one way, the half-sundered torso the other.

Valerius whirled on his toes, quick and fierce as a jungle cat, glaring about for Salome. She must have exhausted her fire dust in the prison. She was bending over Taramis, grasping her sister's black locks in one hand, in the other lifting a dagger. Then with a fierce cry, Valerius' sword was sheathed in her breast with such fury that the point sprang out between her shoulders. With an awful shriek the witch sank down, writhing in convulsions, grasping at the naked blade as it was withdrawn, smoking and dripping. Her eyes were unhuman; with a more than human vitality she clung to the life that ebbed through the wound that split the crimson crescent on her ivory bosom. She groveled on the floor, clawing and biting at the naked stones in her agony.

Sickened at the sight, Valerius stooped and lifted the half-fainting queen. Turning his back on the twisting figure upon the floor, he ran toward the door, stumbling in his haste. He staggered out upon the portico, halted at the head of the steps. The square thronged with people. Some had come at Ivga's incoherent cries; others had deserted the walls in fear of the onsweeping hordes out of the desert, fleeing unreasoningly toward the center of the city. Dumb resignation had vanished. The throng seethed and milled, yelling and screaming. About the road there sounded somewhere the splintering of stone and timbers.

A band of grim Shemites cleft the crowd—the guards of the northern gates, hurrying toward the south gate to reinforce their comrades there. They reined up short at sight of the youth on the steps, holding the limp, naked figure in his arms. The heads of the throng turned toward the temple; the crowd gaped, a new bewilderment added to their swirling confusion.

"Here is your queen!" yelled Valerius, straining to

make himself understood above the clamor. The people gave back a bewildered roar. They did not understand, and Valerius sought in vain to lift his voice above their bedlam. The Shemites rode toward the temple steps, beating a way through the crowd with their spears.

Then a new, grisly element introduced itself into the frenzy. Out of the gloom of the temple behind Valerius wavered a slim white figure, laced with crimson. The people screamed; there in the arms of Valerius hung the woman they thought their queen; yet there in the temple door staggered another figure, like a reflection of the other. Their brains reeled. Valerius felt his blood congeal as he stared at the swaying witch-girl. His sword had transfixed her, sundered her heart. She should be dead; by all laws of nature she should be dead. Yet there she swayed, on her feet, clinging horribly to life.

"Thaug!" she screamed, reeling in the doorway. "*Thaug!*" As in answer to that frightful invocation there boomed a thunderous croaking from within the temple, the snapping of wood and metal.

"That is the queen!" roared the captain of the Shemites, lifting his bow. "Shoot down the man and the other woman!"

But the roar of a roused hunting pack rose from the people; they had guessed the truth at last, understood Valerius' frenzied appeals, knew that the girl who hung limply in his arms was their true queen. With a soul-shaking yell they surged on the Shemites, tearing and smiting with tooth and nail and naked hands, with the desperation of hard-pent fury loosed at last. Above them Salome swayed and tumbled down the marble stair, dead at last.

Arrows flickered about him as Valerius ran back between the pillars of the portico, shielding the body of the queen with his own. Shooting and slashing ruthlessly, the mounted Shemites were holding their own with the maddened crowd. Valerius darted to the temple door—with one foot on the threshold he recoiled, crying out in horror and despair.

Out of the gloom at the other end of the great hall, a vast dark form heaved up—came rushing toward him in gigantic froglike hops. He saw the gleam of great unearthly eyes, the shimmer of fangs or talons. He fell back from the door, and then the whir of a shaft past his ear warned him that death was also behind him. He wheeled desperately. Four or five Shemites had cut their way through the throng and were spurring their horses up the steps, their bows lifted to shoot him down. He sprang behind a pillar, on which the arrows splintered. Taramis had fainted. She hung like a dead woman in his arms.

Before the Shemites could loose again, the doorway was blocked by a gigantic shape. With affrighted yells the mercenaries wheeled and began beating a frantic way through the throng, which crushed back in sudden, galvanized horror, trampling one another in their stampede.

But the monster seemed to be watching Valerius and the girl. Squeezing its vast, unstable bulk through the door, it bounded toward him, as he ran down the steps. He felt it looming behind him, a giant shadowy thing, like a travesty of nature cut out of the heart of night, a black shapelessness in which only the staring eyes and gleaming fangs were distinct.

There came a sudden thunder of hoofs; a rout of Shemites, bloody and battered, streamed across the square from the south, plowing blindly through the packed throng. Behind them swept a horde of horsemen yelling in a familiar tongue, waving red swords—the exiles, returned! With them rode fifty black-bearded desert riders, and at their head a giant figure in black mail.

"Conan!" shrieked Valerius. "*Conan!*"

The giant yelled a command. Without checking their

headlong pace, the desert men lifted their bows, drew and loosed. A cloud of arrows sang across the square, over the seething heads of the multitudes, and sank feather-deep in the black monster. It halted, wavered, reared, a black blot against the marble pillars. Again the sharp cloud sang, and yet again, and the horror collapsed and rolled down the steps, as dead as the witch who had summoned it out of the night of ages.

Conan drew rein beside the portico, leaped off. Valerius had laid the queen on the marble, sinking beside her in utter exhaustion. The people surged about, crowding in. The Cimmerian cursed them back, lifted her dark head, pillowed it against his mailed shoulder.

"By Crom, what is this? The real Taramis! But who is that yonder?"

"The demon who wore her shape," panted Valerius.

Conan swore heartily. Ripping a cloak from the shoulders of a soldier, he wrapped it about the naked queen. Her long dark lashes quivered on her cheeks; her eyes opened, stared up unbelievingly into the Cimmerian's scarred face.

"Conan!" Her soft fingers caught at him. "Do I dream? She told me you were dead——"

"Scarcely!" He grinned widely. "You do not dream. You are queen of Khauran again. I broke Constantius, out there by the river. Most of his dogs never lived to reach the walls, for I gave orders that no prisoners be taken—except Constantius. The city guard closed the gate in our faces, but we burst it in with rams swung from our saddles. I left all my wolves outside, except this fifty. I didn't trust them in here, and these Khaurani lads were enough for the gate guards."

"It has been a nightmare!" she whimpered. "Oh, my poor people! You must help me try to repay them for all they have suffered, Conan, henceforth councillor as well as captain!"

Conan laughed, but shook his head. Rising, he set the queen upon her feet, and beckoned to a number of his Khaurani horsemen who had not continued the pursuit of the fleeing Shemites. They sprang from their horses, eager to do the bidding of their new-found queen.

"No, lass, that's over with. I'm chief of the Zuagirs now and must lead them to plunder the Turanians, as I promised. This lad, Valerius, will make you a better captain than I. I wasn't made to dwell among marble walls, anyway. But I must leave you now and complete what I've begun. Shemites still live in Khauran."

As Valerius started to follow Taramis across the square toward the palace, through a lane opened by the wildly cheering multitude, he felt a soft hand slipped timidly into his sinewy fingers and turned to receive the slender body of Ivga in his arms. He crushed her to him and drank her kisses with the gratitude of a weary fighter who has attained rest at last through tribulation and storm.

But not all men seek rest and peace; some are born with the spirit of the storm in their blood, restless harbingers of violence and bloodshed, knowing no other path. . . .

The sun was rising. The ancient caravan road was thronged with white-robed horsemen, in a wavering line that stretched from the walls of Khauran to a spot far out in the plain. Conan the Cimmerian sat at the head of that column, near the jagged end of a wooden beam that stuck up out of the ground. Near that stump rose a heavy cross, and on that cross a man hung by spikes through his hands and feet.

"Seven months ago, Constantius," said Conan, "it was I who hung there, and you who sat here."

Constantius did not reply; he licked his gray lips and his eyes were glassy with pain and fear. Muscles writhed like cords along his lean body.

"You are more fit to inflict torture than to endure it," said Conan tranquilly. "I hung there on a cross as you are hanging, and I lived, thanks to circumstances and a stamina peculiar to barbarians. But you civilized men are soft; your lives are not nailed to your spines as are ours. Your fortitude consists mainly in inflicting torment, not in enduring it. You will be dead before sundown. And so, Falcon of the desert, I leave you to the companionship of another bird of the desert."

He gestured toward the vultures whose shadows swept across the sands as they wheeled overhead. From the lips of Constantius came an inhuman cry of despair and horror.

Conan lifted his reins and rode toward the river that shone like silver in the morning sun. Behind him the white-clad riders struck into a trot; the gaze of each, as he passed a certain spot, turned impersonally and with the desert man's lack of compassion, toward the cross and the gaunt figure that hung there, black against the sunrise. Their horses' hooves beat out a knell in the dust. Lower and lower swept the wings of the hungry vultures.

# FANTASY-ADVENTURE'S GREATEST HERO

Readers and critics have long considered the tales of Conan to be among the greatest fantasy-adventure epics of all time, comparable to E. R. Eddison, J. R. R. Tolkien and Edgar Rice Burroughs. Lancer is proud to present the complete Conan series in uniform editions. The first ten titles are:

| | | |
|---|---|---|
| CONAN | 74-958 | 75¢ |
| CONAN THE ADVENTURER | 73-526 | 60¢ |
| CONAN THE WARRIOR | 73-549 | 60¢ |
| CONAN THE CONQUEROR | 73-572 | 60¢ |
| CONAN THE USURPER | 73-599 | 60¢ |
| CONAN THE AVENGER | 73-780 | 60¢ |
| CONAN OF THE ISLES | 73-800 | 60¢ |
| CONAN THE FREEBOOTER | 74-963 | 75¢ |
| CONAN THE WANDERER | 74-976 | 95¢ |
| CONAN OF CIMMERIA | 75-072 | 95¢ |

Look for the special display of these titles at your local newsstand or book store. If not available there, send the price of each book you desire, plus 10¢ per book to cover mailing costs, to LANCER BOOKS, INC., 1560 Broadway, New York, N.Y. 10036. On orders of four or more books, Lancer will pay the postage.